Crona Temple

I0661448

The Glorious Return

Outlook

Crona Temple

The Glorious Return

1. Auflage | ISBN: 978-3-73262-746-2

Erscheinungsort: Frankfurt am Main, Deutschland

Erscheinungsjahr: 2018

Outlook Verlag GmbH, Frankfurt.

THE GLORIOUS RETURN.

ARNAUD POINTING TO THE VAUDOIS HILLS. See page 110.

THE GLORIOUS RETURN

A Story of the Vaudois in 1689

BY
CRONA TEMPLE
Author of "The Last House in London," etc.

THE RELIGIOUS TRACT SOCIETY,
56, PATERNOSTER ROW; 65, ST. PAUL'S CHURCHYARD,
AND 164, PICCADILLY.

PREFACE.

I⊤ is nearly two hundred years since the long persecutions of the Church in the Alpine valleys ended in their 'Glorious Return' from exile, and their gain of liberty of conscience and freedom from the yoke of Rome. It is but right that in 1889 Protestant countries should unite in offering sympathy and brotherly help to the Waldensian Church in its time of commemoration. Two hundred years ago, Britain, Germany, Holland, Switzerland, and the Protestants of France vied with each other in showing their generous love for these sorely-tried children of God. And in these happier times it is well to turn back the history page, to learn what it was that stirred the hearts of our forefathers; to learn what manner of woe it was that the Vaudois endured; to read how the God they served did not suffer them to be tempted beyond what they were able to bear, but—giving them the high honour of bearing witness to His truth, He comforted them at last with His gifts of freedom and of peace. It is in such memories that nations may learn their lessons of truest wisdom. Christianity should be national as well as individual: the Heavenly King demands service from nations as well as from hearts. And it is right that, though the Waldenses are foreigners, and a people of but small account on Europe's muster-roll, their bi-centenary should waken echoes in England; such echoes as God wills that noble deeds should stir throughout all time.

THE GLORIOUS RETURN.

CHAPTER I.

T<small>HE</small> sunlight was fading from the hills, and the pine-forests were growing grey in the creeping shadow.

A northerly breeze had been blowing from the mountains, but it had died down, as north winds do, with the sunsetting; a great stillness had fallen upon the valleys.

One could hear the torrent as it leapt from the snows above, rushing and gurgling in the gorge it had graven for itself on its way to the Pélice River. One could hear too, faint and far away, the cry of the ravens as they circled over a meadow; and one might catch the jarring call of a night-hawk as it woke from its daylight sleep.

But these sounds rather blended with than broke upon the silence. And there seemed besides no sign of life or motion in all the width of the valley.

There were traces of cultivation on the hill-sides where careful hands had terraced and tilled the stony soil, winning from the wilderness fields for pastures and for corn.

There were also buildings that had the semblance of cottages, a group of ruins here by the stream-side, and single ones standing yonder beyond the spurs of the pine-woods.

But in those fields were now neither flocks nor herds, nor any sign of corn; and from those broken chimneys no smoke-wreaths drifted to tell of human lives about the warm hearth-stones.

It was the year 1687, and the valley was the Valley of Luserna, in the Piedmontese Alps.

This was the country of the Vaudois, and it was indeed desolate after the bitter persecution which had followed the Revocation of the Edict of Nantes.

Storms of cruelty and the bitterness of superstition had swept the valleys at various times, but never a storm so devastating and terrible as this. From Fenestrelle to Rora, from the Pra Pass to the plains of Piedmont, fire and sword had driven forth the remnant of the Vaudois. Hundreds had fallen, fighting for their faith and for their homes; hundreds had perished under the white pall of the winter snows; and hundreds more had died on the scaffold or in the prisons of the plain.

And the remnant, the poor harried and hunted souls, had gone forth to seek an asylum—if such there might be found—where they might worship their

God according to His Word.

The sun sank lower yet; the line of light retreated farther up the mountain-peaks. The ravens sullenly stooped and settled on the rocks. The torrent kept its noisy way, charged with the blue snow-water that came glancing from the hills.

Suddenly a woman's voice rose on the air, clear, and very sweet. It came through the sprays of creeping plants that veiled a crag so steep that one might marvel how human being could have climbed there. It was a haunt fit only for the chamois or the hill-sheep; and on either hand spread dense forests and ravines where the snow-wreaths lay yet unmelted.

The song rang forth. It was no wavering strain, no uncertain sound, but a chant of triumph that held also a note of defiance—

> 'God's Name is great!
> He breaketh the arrow of the bow
> The shield, the sword and the battle.
> Thou art of more honour and might than the mountains of prey.
> Thou, even Thou art to be feared.
> The earth trembled and was still when God arose
> To help the meek upon the earth.
> The fierceness of man shall turn to Thy praise,
> And the fierceness of the violent shalt Thou restrain.
> God shall refrain the spirit of princes.
> The Lord our God is terrible unto the kings of the earth.'

The voice ceased; as the last note died away the last sun-shaft touched the highest peak. The day was done. Night had fallen on the Valley of Luserna.

Behind the ivy-sprays and the clinging rock plants there was a path on the face of the cliff widening as it rose, until—some fifty feet above the stream—it spread into a platform or tiny amphitheatre completely hidden from any prying eye that might search the cliff from below.

From above one might perhaps peer into its recesses; but then no living thing ever did look from above, save the falcons and the ravens, or perhaps a wild goat, tempted by the tufts of mountain flowers which bloomed against the edges of the snow.

Presently, far back in the hill-cleft, a small red flame leaped up, fed on dried grasses and fir-cones.

'Rénée, Rénée,' called a woman's voice, 'thou art too rash, dear child. May not that light betray us after all?'

'Oh, no, mother! No one comes here now; we are safe, quite safe. And see where Tutu creeps forward to the blaze! Thou art cold, my poor Tutu? Then rest thee, none will harm thee here.'

MAY NOT THAT LIGHT BETRAY?

A dormouse lifted its beadlike eyes to the speaker's face, as if well understanding that it was loved and safe. It was a sort of friend to these poor refugees, here in their mountain hiding-place, a creature even more weak and helpless than themselves.

Again the woman's voice was heard.

'Dear child, be not stubborn. Have we endured so much only to perish now for lack of a little further patience? A fire even by daylight is rash, at night its glow is almost certain to be seen.'

The girl she addressed stood silent for a moment, the flicker of the fire fell on her slender figure and on the graceful lines of her head and throat. Then she stooped and flung earth upon the flame, treading out the scarcely kindled heap, and scattering the fir-cones till their brightened edges died into little rims and coils of grey.

Rénée Janavel had learnt how to obey and how to suffer, but to-night one word of pleading forced its way from her lips.

'It is in the night,' she said, 'in the dark night that we need the cheer and the warmth. Oh, mother, I lit the fire to keep away my fear——'

The words sank in a broken whisper; it was strange for Rénée Janavel to speak of fear.

The woman paused in wonder.

Why should Rénée be afraid of aught but the danger which the blaze might bring—the danger of cruel men who were thirsting for their blood: men who had sworn that no remnant of the proscribed race should be left in the valleys, and who had swept the fields and forests again and again in their search for any Vaudois in hiding there? Renée, child of the mountains as she was, why should she fear anything but this? The winter was past, and the prowling wolves had withdrawn themselves; the shy black bears that haunted the hills were not creatures to be greatly affrighted at. What ailed the girl?

Renée came to her side, and hid her face against the woman's knee.

'It is so lonely,' she murmured brokenly. 'Lately, at night, I have thought over many things, terrible things—and I have been frightened even to turn my head, too frightened to call to you. Oh, mother, mother dear! will these days never have an end? Shall we never be happy again, Gaspard and you and I?

'I know that it is cowardly,' she went on in pathetic appeal. 'But, mother, you are well now, almost quite strong again: could we not creep away and gain the Swiss country where the rest are gone; and see the dear friendly faces, and sleep in peace, afraid of no man?'

She stopped, for her throat was full of sobbing, and her head sank lower yet upon the trembling hands.

Just then some remaining spark of fire was kindled into blaze by the wind that swept into the cave, and the dried grass leapt into a red flame that threw dancing gleams and shadows on the rocks around, and touched the trunk of a pine overhanging the place with a glow as of deepest orange. Little Tutu, the dormouse, curled himself up in soft satisfaction, a nut which Renée had given him held tight in his tiny paws.

The woman looked at the fire, but she did not again ask that it should be extinguished.

'Renée,' she said, 'it is out of all possibility that I should climb the hill passes. I can never see the Swiss country. And, indeed, here in mine own land I would choose to stay, that my last earthly look should rest on the valley I love so well. And for yourself, dear child, how could you go all that long and dangerous way? It was for my sake that you stayed, Renée. But now—I would not keep you, child, if it were possible for you to gain safety, to reach friends, there in the land where one may worship the good God in peace. But as it is——'

'Mother! do not speak so! Never, never can I desert you! You know I will not leave you while life holds us together.'

She rose to her feet. One might see the stateliness of her figure as she stood betwixt the fire-glow and the twilight, her head erect, her face full of the strength of love and trust.

'Sing it again, mother,' she said, 'the hymn that you sang just now. And forget that Rénée has been afraid of shadows.'

The woman took her hand and held it tenderly between her own.

'Tell me, Rénée,' she said, 'why were you frightened? Has any new thing chanced?'

'No, no; it is the long weariness, the uncertainty, the remembering—oh, it is just everything! Whilst you were ill, mother, I had no time to be frightened; but now, when we sit and watch the sun go down, I remember all that has happened, and I turn sick at my very heart.'

She shuddered. They had passed, those two women, through terror enough to try any mortal nerves, and privations sufficient to exhaust the strongest frame. It was small marvel that Rénée trembled as she remembered the past.

'Sing, mother,' she said again; 'Gaspard was always wont to say that your songs uplifted his courage.'

So 'The Psalm of Strong Confidence' was chanted once more, the notes of the woman's voice filling the place with its rich volume of sound. The quick blaze had died down, and the dark shades fell across the cavern. But without, beyond the stooping pines, the sky was brightening. The stars stole out on the deep vault of blue, those glittering stars which tell through all speech and language that the statutes of the Lord are true, and that in keeping of them there is great reward.

And the two women sat, hand in hand, serene in spite of trouble; content, although they were homeless and hunted on the earth. Nay, just now they were more than 'content!' they could rejoice that they, like their martyred ancestors, were found worthy to bear the cross of suffering for their Master's sake.

Rénée Janavel was an orphan. Madeleine Botta, the woman she called 'mother,' was bound to her not by ties of blood, but by the stronger ties of love and gratitude. She had inherited a name which was known throughout the length and breadth of the valleys. Her grandfather, 'the hero of Rora,' Joshua Janavel, had led the patriot bands who battled against enormous odds in the persecution of 1655 and the few following years. Her father had been sentenced by the Inquisition, and if he were not dead, his miserable existence, chained to an oar as a galley-slave, was worse a hundred times for him than death itself.

Her young mother had perished in the prisons of Turin, and Rénée, a mere child when the Duke of Savoy stopped for a time those terrible deeds of blood, had lived always at Rora with the Bottas.

Madeleine Botta had lost her own daughter, and she had taken Rénée to her heart instead, loving and cherishing her until the desolate child almost forgot that Madeleine was not in very truth what she always called her, 'her mother.' And was she not Gaspard's mother? and were not Gaspard's people to be her people? his life, her life? She would have been Gaspard's wife at Easter-tide, had not this new time of death and danger come upon the valleys. Now he was swept off with the fighting men, none exactly could tell whither; and she was here, hidden in the rock-ledges, seeking shelter with Madeleine from the ravaging hordes that had sworn to 'exterminate the heretics as they would exterminate all other sorts of noxious beasts.'

The home at Rora was a heap of ashes; the peaceful days when Rénée drove the goats down the hill in the shadowy afternoon, or sat busily spinning the flax at Madeleine's knee, were gone for ever. There had been troubles then, of course, but troubles so tiny that now in comparison they seemed to be positive pleasures.

Henri Botta, the house-master, was a hard-featured man, whose rare words were sometimes wont to be hard; he looked on the world as a vale of sighing, a place where evil reigned, and no man should desire to be happy. Rénée used to shrink from his warning words, and strive to avoid his grim glances. Now how glad she would have been to have heard the sound of his voice, or to have seen the outline of his rugged face!

Then there was Emile, the eldest son, almost as hard and silent as his father; and even Gaspard had a trick of shutting his lips tightly together and frowning till his black brows met, when the talk was of the future or the past.

But Gaspard had never been hard to Rénée—never. He had been to Turin learning his trade, a carpenter he was, and the best carpenter, as Rénée proudly said, in all the commune. He was away for years, for such delicate work as his is not learned in a hurry, and on his return he found the child Rénée grown into a fair and gracious maiden, the realisation of the dreams which had haunted his young manhood.

And so he loved her, and wooed her, and won her; learning from her gentleness to unbend his sternness, teaching her girlish heart to be staunch and earnest.

They had built and plenished their future home in the simple fashion of the valley folk. Rénée was already stitching at the wedding gear, and Madeleine Botta had proudly piled the homespun linen which was to be her marriage gift to the girl who was already as her dear daughter.

And then—

But the tale is dark in the telling. One must go back some way in Europe's history to understand how such deeds came to be done, how such devastation fell ever and again on the devoted people of the Vaudois valleys.

RORA.

CHAPTER II.

THERE are sad pages in all histories: there are tales in every land the telling of which must awaken deep feelings of horror. Man's inhumanity to man has always been the dark stain upon God's earth.

But no cruelties of the ancient days—not even the ghastly enormities of Nero or the evil deeds of the 'dark ages'—can exceed the terror and trouble, the fiendish works, the rage and oppression which have reigned in the Vaudois valleys.

From primitive times those valleys in the Savoy Alps have been the refuge of Christians who only asked to be allowed to live, harmless and insignificant, tending their mulberry trees, their vineyards and their corn; with liberty to serve God according to the simple faith which had been handed down to them from their fathers. They had books which they greatly prized,—portions of God's Word, poems, commentaries, and their own *Noble Lesson*. This celebrated book was written or compiled about the year 1100, in the Romance language,—and in this language they also possessed the text of the Psalms and several books of the Old and New Testaments.

They themselves declared that it was the persecutions of the Roman emperors which had driven the first Christian settlers to the valleys; and if it were so the little Church, born of persecution and nourished by martyrdom, had learned from the first to endure all things as good soldiers of its Master, Christ.

From the earliest times there have always been faithful hearts humbly following the steps of the Lord, seeking, above earthly wealth and weal, to know and to do God's will. And such there will ever be until the Master comes again. Evil may seem triumphant, and pride and arrogance lift prosperous fronts, but the Lord knoweth them that are His, and there shall never lack a remnant to watch and wait for Him.

It is not needful to trace in this story the growth of the pomp and power of the Bishop of Rome, nor to tell at length how the 'successor' of St. Peter ceased to be either humble or faithful. The Empire of the West had crumbled away, the ancient seat of the Cæsars was empty, and gradually the bishop became the most important person in the city, claiming one thread of power after another until the 'Sovereign Pontiff' asserted rule and right over the length and breadth of Christendom.

It was strange that such pretensions could be based on the Gospel of Him who took on Himself the form of a servant, and whose first words of teaching were a blessing on the 'poor in spirit.' Perhaps it was partly a dim consciousness of this that made pope and cardinals wish the people not to read the writings of the apostles and the words of the Lord.

But reading in those days was no easy matter.

Books were scarce and costly. Learning was difficult. The bulk of the people only heard God's Word through the mouths of those whose gain it was to suppress and distort its simple teaching. Men and women lived and died believing that pope and priest could forgive sins and wipe off all offences, and that a handful of gold pieces could purchase their entrance into paradise.

It was through these dark days that the Light of the Truth burned clear in the hearts and homes of the simple race dwelling on the confines of Savoy, where the frontier lines of Switzerland and France met on the white-hill peaks. And this race it was, this 'nest of heretics,' that the Roman power resolved to crush and kill.

The first persecution that was regularly organised to destroy them root and branch took place at the end of the twelfth century. In addition to those slain outright, the number of those carried into captivity was so great that the Archbishop of Avignon declared that he had 'so many prisoners it is impossible not only to defray the charge of their nourishment, but to get enough lime and stone to build prisons for them.'

From this time onwards the history of valleys is one long tale of persecution. The intervals when 'the churches had rest, and were edified,' were so short that the accounts of suffering and martyrdom must have been handed down verbally from father to son. Thirty-two invasions were endured, invasions of troops filled with the remorseless rage of religious fanaticism.

But it was in the year 1650 that the bitterest storm broke over them. It was a time of extraordinary 'religious' feeling, and councils were established in Turin and other cities, having for their object the spread of the Romish faith and the utter extirpation of heretics. The plan on which they worked was just the old barbarous way of force and fire, and the worst weapon of all, treachery.

Once again the Vaudois fled before the soldiers hired to butcher them. The caves and dens of the rocks, the mountain passes filled with snows that April suns had no power to melt, the natural fastnesses and citadels of the hills— these were the places to which the villagers escaped. And as they went they were lighted by the blaze of their burning homesteads, and followed by the shrieks and groans of the weak and their helpless defenders, whom the ruthless murderers overtook, tortured and slew.

It was then that Janavel of Rora came to the front. He had but six men with him when he first made a stand on the heights above Villaro, where the mountain track leads over the Collina di Rabbi to Rora. He lay in ambush, resolved to do what he could to stop the foreign soldiers from ravaging his home, and in his desperate mood he had no thought save to sell his life as dearly as he could: what could seven men do against hundreds?

But in that narrow place seven men could do much. The simultaneous discharge of their muskets threw the soldiers into confusion. No enemy was to be seen; the troops could not be sure that those rocks and trees did not shelter scores of Vaudois. They faltered, then fell back.

Again the musket-balls came crashing from the hill-side. It was more than hired courage could stand! The troops of Savoy turned and fled, leaving sixty or seventy of their number dead on the ground.

They fled only to return. The next day six hundred picked men ascended the mountain by the Cassutee, a wider, more practicable path. But here also Janavel was ready for them. He had now gathered eighteen herdsmen, some armed with muskets and pistols, but the greater number having only slings and flint stones, which they knew very well how to use. Their ambush was well chosen. The column advanced, only to be assailed flank and front with a shower of balls and stones. Again this invisible foe was too much for them to stand. They thought only of escaping from the fatal defile; once more Janavel was victorious.

The Marquis of Pianezza, the Savoy leader, was furious at these repulses. He hastily collected his whole force, sending for his lieutenant, the impetuous and cruel Mario, to bring up the rear-guard, together with some bands of Irish mercenaries, who were specially fit for dashing and dangerous service. Rora should surely be carried this time! Every soul there should rue the hour in which they had dared to oppose Pianezza!

But Janavel and his heroes were armed with a strength on which the foe had little calculated. For the third time victory rested with the weak. For the third time the soldiers were driven down the mountain-slopes, hurling one another to destruction in their mad flight.

But this could not last for ever. Eight thousand soldiers and two thousand popish peasants were marched on Rora, and this time the work of death was done.

Janavel and his friends, who had been decoyed to a distance from the village, escaped with their lives, and for many weeks they carried on the struggle, only to be beaten at last, overpowered by numbers. But the name of Janavel was reverenced far and wide as that of a good man, 'bold as a lion, meek as a lamb,' rendering to God alone the praise of his victories, dauntless in his faith and love, while tried as few are tried. His wife and daughter had fallen into the hands of Pianezza,—spared for the time from the massacre at Rora; a letter from the general reached Janavel, offering him his life, and their lives, if he would abjure his heresy, but threatening him with death and his dear ones with being burnt alive if he persisted in his resistance. 'We are in God's hands,' answered Janavel; 'our bodies may die by your means, but our souls will serve Him by the grace that He gives to us. Tempt me no more.'

And much the same he wrote thirty years after, when he and Pastor Arnaud planned the Glorious Return.

It was no marvel that Renée, Gaspard Botta's betrothed wife, blushed as she spoke of fear. The blood of her heroic grandsire ran in her veins. She too could trust in God, and for His sake endure.

There was a time of peace after that terrible persecution. The whole of Protestant Europe had remonstrated against the cruelties and horrors that had taken place. Oliver Cromwell, then governing England, sent an ambassador to Turin to enforce, if possible, his indignant demand for mercy. Holland, Switzerland, the German Protestant powers, and even a large number of French subjects, all sent messengers to the Duke of Savoy. And they sent also large sums—more than a million francs—to relieve the most pressing necessities of the homeless and the destitute.

The Duke of Savoy died, and under the rule of his son, Victor Amadeus II., the Vaudois had some years of peace. They showed their gratitude for this forbearance by loyally defending the frontier against the Genoese, and by eagerly helping to quell the banditti infesting the mountain passes. They sought to prove, with a devotion that borders upon pathos, that they also could be good subjects, that their allegiance to their God only heightened their loyalty to their sovereign.

It was then that Renée Janavel sang as she sewed the long seams in the linen store that her foster-mother had spun. It was then that Gaspard would whistle as his plane cut through the white plank, and the shavings fell, silky and shining, about his feet.

Even the grim house-master would let the suspicion of a smile lurk under the straight moustache of iron-grey that almost hid his lips. He could remember the times of terror—oh, yes, he could remember them only too well!—but ferns and wreaths of mauve auricula were now growing about the ruins that had then been made so fearsome; and the mulberries were flourishing again; and it was a comfort to see Mother Madeleine about and well after her sharp attack of fever a year or two ago; and Emile and Gaspard had grown sturdy and strong—the finest young men in all Rora; and Rénée—the child—was always singing when she was not laughing: what a gay, sweet heart it was, to be sure! And, all things considered, it was no marvel that Henri Botta now and then forgot all the ghastly doings of the past, and let a smile dawn upon his lips or glimmer in his eyes.

GASPARD AND RENEE.

'Shall it be in the spring time, dear?' Gaspard said, as he stood in the house that his hands had builded for his bride, and let his glance rest lovingly on her bright face. 'Say, dear, shall we light our fire on this hearth when the snows melt on Mount Friolent, and the flowers bloom under the hedges yonder?'

If she did not answer him in words, he was nevertheless well contented. And it was settled that so it should be: for not even the neighbours could disapprove of such a marriage. Were not the two born for each other? he so strong and dark and staunch, and she so fair and sweet! And was not Gaspard the best workman in the commune, with his earnings all safely saved since he came back from Turin?

Why should there not be a marriage procession along the stream-side to the little white-walled church when the flowers bloomed? Why not, indeed? And wide and long should be the festive wreaths woven of those very flowers to do honour to the grandchild of the hero Janavel.

It was the close of the year 1685. There had been twenty years of freedom in the valleys—twenty calm years of liberty and peace. The horrid sounds of massacre had died away before Rénée was old enough to remember, before Gaspard was old enough to understand. And so they looked into one another's eyes, and thought that life and love and earth and heaven were smiling on their troth.

16

But far away, beyond the French Alps, beyond the vineyards of Burgundy and the Lyonais, an old man sat in his splendid palace, a wretched and restless man, who had something to say to the plans and the promises of the simple folk in the Savoy valleys.

For he was King Louis XIV., Louis, surnamed the Great, Louis, the husband of the bigot Françoise de Maintenon, trying in his old age of repentance to atone for the guilt of a misspent life. Madame de Maintenon hated heretics as her cold, calculating heart hated nothing else; and she loved the approval and the flattery of her courtier priests far more than she loved the king.

'Revoke the edicts giving liberty to the Protestants, sire,' she said to her husband. 'Crush heresy, and so purchase your peace with God.'

Louis listened. He was aged and ailing; his sons were dead; his friends— such friends as he had—were dead too. He also must soon appear before the Throne that was greater even than the glories of his own. It was time he hearkened to the promptings of the Church. Popes and priests must know best about these things; he would do their bidding, and do it thoroughly, as a king should!

So the edicts were revoked throughout the land of France. All the civil rights of his subjects belonging to the Reformed faith were taken away. The heretics must be converted, or go, or die.

Thus he ordered.

And even then, not quite content, he forced his neighbour, the young Duke of Savoy, to do likewise. To the valleys also the persecution should extend.

…   …   ·   ·

And Gaspard set his teeth hard as he brightened up his father's sword; and Rénée's tears fell fast as she folded away the snowy linen she had bleached so fair.

GASPARD SHARPENING HIS SWORD.

When the violets bloomed in the hedges long processions passed that were different indeed from marriage-trains. Trumpet-calls and the tramp of troops echoed from the hills and rocks; and the white walls of the church had been splashed with crimson, and were now blackened with fire.

Once more Rome had sent her 'terror' to the valleys. Once more faith was to be tried to the death, and steadfast souls to win their martyr crowns.

CHAPTER III.

VICTOR AMADEUS did not obey King Louis without a struggle. He was content with his Vaudois subjects; they were industrious and law-abiding, and they were a valuable defence against invasion from the west, and a check upon the bandits of the Alps. Why should he harry and hunt them forth to soothe the sore conscience of that tyrannical old man in Versailles?

But the French ambassador put the matter in a light which speedily convinced Victor Amadeus. His master, he said, King Louis, had resolved that heresy should be stamped utterly out. He would send an army to the Savoy valleys, an army quite strong enough to accomplish the purpose. The Duke of Savoy need not trouble himself at all. The work should be done, and thoroughly done, by the French alone, but—and the addition had a strong and grave significance—but the King of France would retain the Piedmont valleys for his trouble!

What could Duke Victor say? These Vaudois, after all, were heretics; his own father had done exactly what King Louis was now urging upon him to do; hesitation might be another name for lukewarmness in a holy cause. And at all risks he must avoid giving Louis an excuse for making good his footing on the soil of Savoy.

Therefore the proclamation was signed.

A terrible proclamation it was. It ordained complete cessation of every religious service, save that of the Romish faith; the immediate destruction of the churches; the banishment of the pastors, and the baptism of every child by Romish priests, who were henceforth to educate and control all young people.

The punishment for disobeying or evading this edict was death.

Dismay entered all hearts. Rome was once more to whet her savage sword. And the mountaineers, helpless, defenceless, could only die, since submission to such edicts could not be.

They remembered 1655, and the way in which a handful of men had beaten back Pianezza and his hordes.

The courage that had nerved Janavel and his heroes was still alight in the valleys. They too would fight for their homes and their churches, for the honour of their wives, for the faith of their little ones.

So entrenchments were thrown up in the ravines, and turf and rough stones piled up on every point of vantage; stores were hastily collected, and the corn-stacks were threshed out. The women did their part; even the children were busy as bees.

Henri Botta heard the careless laughter of a string of boys and girls as they ran up the steps of the mill, carrying each one a burden of wheat or rye, and his grave face grew sterner still as he harkened.

'Little they know! little they know!' he muttered in his beard. 'Laugh! 'tis the last laughter that will sound in Luserna for many and many a day.'

The horrors of the months that followed cannot here be told. Is it not an awful thing that men have committed atrocities of which one cannot speak—that living bodies and tortured souls have borne what our ears cannot suffer to hear—what our minds cannot endure to conceive? Frail women, modest and gentle girls, the babies too young to know the terror of the sword that slew them, the old men whose white hairs were but signals for scoff and insult—all these helpless ones were the butt and playthings of the brutal soldiers, whose most merciful dealing was death. Aye, happy were those whose doom was *only* death!

Botta and his two sons fought at the barricade which crossed the road above Casiana. Emile was amongst the first to fall. His father saw him stagger, and rushed forward to his help; but, as he reached upwards to where Emile lay on the ridge of the earthwork, a second ball crashed into the prostrate figure. The boy was shot through the heart.

'Let him lie there,' muttered Botta, with a quietude more sad than tears. 'Let him lie there, on the crest of the barricade Even in death he shall defend the valleys.'

Yet the heroism and devotion so lavishly poured out in those days and weeks of struggle were in vain. Once more the valleys were swept from north to south, from the Palavas Alps to the Po River—once more the red flames raged and triumphed above the cottage roofs; and over the fields, and by the swift torrent water, the flying people were hunted down and slain.

It was the end of April, 1686. The home of the Bottas was a blackened heap of ruin; the orchards, where the tufts of pink apple-blossom should be already showing, were hacked and hewed away, and the down-trodden vines lay in long trailing lines amid the wrecks of the village.

A few soldiers lounged and laughed in their encampments hard by; they were roasting a goat that they had shot for their supper, and their rude jokes as they did so roused noisy mirth. Their task of blood and cruelty had brutalized them to a degree hard to believe, did not one know how low human nature can fall when riot and licence cut away the cords of gentleness and justice, and the blood-thirst is awakened—that thirst which men share with the tigers.

Henri, the house-master, was gone from Rora; where, none could tell, for the Vaudois troops had been scattered like clouds before the tempest. Gaspard had come back alone, creeping up the passes in the night, hiding, and groping his dangerous way, to find out what had befallen his mother and Rénée.

He knew every nook and crevice of the ridges that rose grim and almost inaccessible between the ravine and Villaro; somewhere hereabouts he hoped to find them, unless—indeed——

And the young man's haggard eyes gleamed with the look that it is ill to see on mortal face as he counted out what that 'unless' might mean.

His search was long, and his heart grew heavier hour by hour. Perhaps they had already been driven off to prison in Turin; or, perhaps—and if he were not to find them Gaspard knew that he ought to pray that it might be so— perhaps they had already joined Emile in the land where fighting and desolation and death is over for ever, where God Himself will give comfort and the calmness of His peace.

The dawn was breaking, the glad, sweet dawn of the spring morning, and Gaspard slowly dragged himself beneath the shelter of the pines. He must not stand there, exposed, under those shafts of clear, keen light, unless he were willing to take his chance of a musket-ball from the duke's soldiers, whose orders were to clear the country as a broom sweeps over a floor.

There was a cavern here, up under the cliff, a place where he might lie and rest, and eat the crust of bread he carried in his wallet. Rest—food—they were sorely needed, yet he felt as though rest were impossible, and food would choke him.

GASPARD AT THE CAVE.

He lifted the ivy trails and stood a moment, peering into the dimness. These mountain caves held strange creatures now and then.

From out of the darkness came a sudden cry.

'O Gaspard, O Gaspard! is it thou?'

He staggered. He was worn and faint, and just at that moment the hope was dim of finding those he sought. His brain whirled round; he put his hand to his eyes, bewildered.

Then a woman's arms reached out to him, and confused words, and little cries of joy, and short sobs came in broken gusts and silences.

'Gaspard! Oh, thanks be to God! Thou art living then, Gaspard! Mother, mother, awake! here is he, our Gaspard.' And Rénée clung to him and hid her face against his breast.

They were safe then, as yet! And his voice came back to him as he knelt to kiss his mother's hand and cheek. Ah, the swords of the duke were sharp, the desolation of the valleys was drear, the house-father was an exile, and Emile lay in his gory grave; but an offering of heartfelt praise went up to God's throne as the re-united ones held each other's hands and thanked the Lord that day.

There was much to hear on either side, and the women's faces grew very grave when Gaspard told them what had happened in the valleys of Luserna and Angrogna. Cannon and cavalry had been too much for the mountaineers in the villages and on the roads, and treachery had beguiled them from the entrenchments on the heights to which they had fled. The Savoy general had offered, in the duke's name, safe and honourable treatment for themselves, their wives, and children, if they would throw themselves on their conquerer's clemency. The words were fair, the terms all they dared expect. They trusted the promise and laid down their arms.

How their trust was betrayed is a long and shameful tale. Some were led in chains to the fortresses of the plains, some were executed then and there, many were destroyed by the brutal soldiers, and two thousand little children were handed over to Roman Catholic families to be trained in that religion.

Thus it was that Victor Amadeus conquered—for the same thing had occurred in all the valleys, although Gaspard only knew what had happened near at home. Perosa and San Martino had been treated with like barbarity and deceit. The scenes at the rocks of Vadolin were to the full as heart-rending as what Gaspard could describe.

'And thy father?' Madeleine's eyes asked the question which her lips could scarcely frame. 'Thy father, what of him?'

Gaspard rose to his feet and leant against the rock where the dark cave-shadow almost hid his countenance.

'Ah,' he said, 'I have been well-nigh torn in twain betwixt my desire to find you, to know that thou and Rénée were out of the clutches of yon——'

'Name them not, my son,' said Madeleine; 'hard words hurt only the heart from which they come.'

'Words? Aye, it is not with words I would meet them!' the young man said between his teeth.

'And thy father?'

'He is wounded. He was thrust at with a lance when trying to defend Marie Rozel. You remember old Marie? the widow who gave us goat's milk when we were lost in the hill-mist long ago, Emile and I, and Rénée—thou wert a tiny child then, Rénée. They—well, they killed her at last, in spite of all that my father could do.'

'Where is he?' Madeleine Botta had come close to her son and was holding his arm. 'Oh, Gaspard, ill, wounded as he is, surely he is not alone? Let us go to him.'

'Mother, to cross the valley, to go down by the river in broad daylight—it is death, certain death, or worse. Nay, I will creep back to him, and bring him word how you fare. He will revive when once he knows that you and Rénée are safe. It was to get news for him that I am come. But how have you lived here? Have you food? fire?'

So they showed him their store, the bag of rye-bread Rénée had stolen down to Rora to fetch from a secret hiding-place; the dried grapes, the chestnuts, the flour—which last was useless, since they dared not light a fire; and then, stepping forward, the girl called softly once and again. Presently two or three goats came pushing their way through the ivy, rustling beneath the glossy leaves, and nodding their sage sharp heads as they came.

'The others have been killed, I suppose,' said Rénée sadly; 'but these give us milk enough and to spare.'

Gaspard watched her as she stroked the creatures that were pressing against her knees. All dumb things seemed ready to love Rénée, and it was no wonder.

Madeleine sat silently. Her heart was full; her lips were quivering; the iron was entering her very soul. God had required much from her—her happy home, the quiet contentment of her failing years; then the life of Emile, her eldest born; and now Henri, the husband of her youth, her strong Henri, was stricken. Was his life to be taken too?

This woman had come of a race of martyrs: she had been cradled in terror, and reared amongst dangers and blood-spilling. She knew, none better, what it meant to take up Christ's cross and follow Him along the path that leads to where the shadow lies across the shining Threshold. Her nature was brave, as befitted a child of the hills; her soul was filled with a high and sacred faith that had been lighted by God's Gospel and nourished by His grace.

But now, there, in the cavern, the grief, the pity, the despair of it well-nigh overcame her.

'O Lord, how long, how long? Must Thy people be outcasts for ever? for ever down-trodden and slain? Canst Thou not hear in heaven Thy dwelling-place, and when Thou hearest wilt Thou not aid?'

Just now, in her hour of agony and sore dismay, she was too near to pain to see its glorious crown, too close to the shadow of death to behold the shining gate. Not only for her and hers that crown and shining should be, but for ever unto the uttermost ages the Church of Christ is fairer for what then the Vaudois bore! Not a tear nor drop of martyr blood fell then unmarked, for not only on earth but in heaven is the death of God's saints held 'right dear.'

CHAPTER IV.

Renee, if God gives me life, I will return; I will return here to thee.'

So said Gaspard Botta as he parted from his promised wife in the cavern on the cliff.

He had stayed long enough to gather them a store of wood and firing. He had even crept down in the darkness to the ruined home, and, with the silent hunter-craft of his nation, had managed to evade the Savoy soldiers while he loaded himself with things which he knew his mother and Rénée must need.

A dangerous service—yes, but existence was just one long course of danger in those months to the Vaudois.

Madeleine had urged him to go back to his father. She herself would have chosen to dare all things, and go also. To stay in that cliff-cage, hiding in silence, with no knowledge of how it fared with her nearest and dearest, would be a terrible strain and trial; the risks of crossing the Luserna valley and the heights of Roussina and Mount Vandalin, watched as they were by the duke's troops, would be as nothing compared with the waiting and the longing for news there in the cave.

But Gaspard, who had threaded the passes and forded the torrents swelled with melting snows, who had doubled and dived and scrambled like the hunted thing that he was, implored her to stay in the comparative safety of their hiding-place.

'It is far to where I left him,' he said; 'out there below La Vachère. And if thou didst reach him, mother, they would but tear thee from his side. The men were driven off in gangs to Luserna, and the women——' He paused, and the dark look came again into his face. 'The women were taken too, some of them, and the little ones—— Oh, mother, be satisfied! rest here, thou and Rénée, and if God pleases to hear my prayer I will come again, and bring my father, should I carry him on my shoulders.'

And so he left them; and for days, and yet again for days, they watched and waited for his coming back across the torrent, and round by the huge rocks that rose sharp and sheer from the water to the fringes of the pines. But they waited in vain.

And as the time wore on they saw from their point of vantage that the soldiers had left Rora, or only scoured the land at intervals; and Renée ventured down from time to time to the desolated village, filling her basket with such fruits and food that the ruthless robbers had chanced to spare. Seeking, too, if there might be other fugitives perhaps more helpless and terror-stricken than themselves—to whom Madeleine and she could give a word of cheer or hand of help.

And so the spring deepened into summer, and the skies were stainless blue above them; and the sunlight of many blossoms shone over the grass; the pines shook their yellow dust in clouds into the scented air; and the brooms opened their dry seed-pods with sharp reports, as of fairy artillery.

It was hard to believe that only so few weeks ago human lives had been sobbed out in agony—there in that beautiful world—and that rage and cruelty had wrought their worst wickedness in the sacred name of Christ.

So quiet was it, that at last the two women went back to Rora, finding shelter amongst the ruins of what had once been their home. One or two other hunted and bereaved ones crept back also, like them waiting for news, hoping still in their faithful hearts that better times would come, and those so dear to them would be delivered from the jaws of death.

Renée would look wistfully northward and westward, where the great violet peaks rose into the summer sky. Would Gaspard come that day? the next? Deferred hope that maketh the heart sick was heavy upon her; she longed to find her way down the valley to the outer world, and learn for herself what had befallen. Inaction and waiting were the hardest of trials to this girl, child of the mountain as she was.

Patience, Renée! The time for doing will come. The blood of heroes does not flow uselessly in your young veins; 'to do' comes by nature to hearts like yours; 'to wait' is a lesson taught by care Divine.

Some stray reports penetrated even to the far recesses of this valley, the most southern of all the Vaudois dwelling-places. Some wandering folk would come from Vigne or Villaro, outcasts like themselves, whom they might question. Any well-to-do traveller, any body of men, any strangers who looked happy and well-fed, must be avoided and hidden from, for they would certainly prove to be enemies, who considered all the Vaudois to be under the ban of the Church, and therefore to be driven to a Luserna prison, or hunted down and slain.

But from one and another the story was brokenly gathered—the story of what had chanced beyond the hills, and what sort of measure the duke had dealt to his conquered people.

Exile. That had been the final decree.

The Vaudois were to be driven out; their hills should harbour heretics no more. Once and for all Savoy should be cleared from them and their doctrine. As Louis had purified the soil of France, so Victor Amadeus would purge Piedmont.

The prisons were to be emptied. The twelve thousand men, women, and children shut up in the several fortresses must go. To Switzerland, since the Swiss would receive them—but across the Alps, and out of the valleys at any cost, and any whither.

Twelve thousand? Could there really be so many? Henri Botta and his son Gustave were amongst that great and dreary company.

The sentence fell on the hearts of those two women like a leaden weight.

They, too, must go to Switzerland.

That was the resolve that grew strong in each before they dared to say the words one to the other. They were silently counting the miles, the mountains, the dangers that lay between them and the country where their dear ones had been driven. And each dreaded the objections which the other might urge.

'But, Rénée,' Madeleine Botta held out her withered hands imploringly, and her sunken eyes were moist as she spoke—'Rénée, we must go to them, since it may not be that they can come to us.'

The girl's face shone with the swift up-leaping of the hope that was strong in her.

'Yes, mother, we will go; and God will lead us safely through!' was her answer, spoken with the fervent simple faith that had sprung strongly up in Vaudois hearts under that red-rain of martyr blood.

But not yet was the 'leading' to come.

MADELEINE AND RENEE STOPPED.

CHAPTER V.

T<small>HEY</small> set out, their bundles on their shoulders, walking openly in the daylight without attempt at disguise; seeking, it is true, the less frequented paths, and avoiding observation as much as possible. They were so inoffensive, so insignificant, this woman and her foster-child; surely few would notice them or hinder them—now that the bitterness of the persecution had died down.

Sorrowfully were they mistaken.

They had not lost sight of the white ridge of Mount Friolent, nor crested the pass leading toward Villaro, before they were stopped and questioned by a band of preaching friars who were busy establishing their churches and schools in the country whence 'the heretics' had been driven.

Madeleine's courage rose with the first hint of danger. She had no idea of softening or disguising anything, and answered back so dauntlessly that Rénée's cheeks grew white as she listened; though the girl herself had no lack of truth nor of courage. Words are in these nineteenth-century days little else than easily stirred air; to those defenceless ones just then they meant all the difference betwixt life and death.

The friars consulted together and shook their cowled heads, looking not unlike birds of prey gloating over some poor trapped wild thing. They said that the women were firebrands, and far too dangerous to be allowed to go through the land—that the duke allowed none of the so-called Reformed religion to dwell or pass in Piedmont; and that Mistress Botta and the girl must travel in their company to Luserna, 'where further decisions would be arrived at.'

That night the two women found means of escape. They gained the open air, the hills, the steep and intricate ways known only to the people of the valleys; and presently, after some days of wandering, they found themselves once more in their cavern. The tears rolled down Rénée's cheeks as she entered—it was present safety, indeed, but must they still wait there, and watch for the footsteps that might never come—for the news which seemed further from them than ever?

Then Madeleine fell sick. Some slow fever consumed her; and for days and nights she lay so ill that Rénée could find no place in her thoughts for aught but 'mother.' And when at last she seemed to revive somewhat, and her wandering reason returned to her, she was so exceeding weak and frail that the girl feared she would die from very weariness.

It was hard to get necessaries, harder still to obtain the food fitted for a sick woman's needs, but Rénée never flagged nor faltered all through that terrible time.

She drove the straying goats from the mountain, that her mother might have draughts of their milk; she managed to make charcoal of her store of dry wood, and that so carefully that no volume of smoke or flame could betray their hiding-place. She ran down to the valley for the few bunches of grapes which might yet be left on the broken and neglected vines; and once, but only once, she dared to enter the village of Rumero, where she bartered her own long silver chain for a warm coverlet for Madeleine.

And the autumn came, and the winter. And the icicles had been hung across their cave, and the raging winds had careered there, while the avalanches thundered amongst the higher Alps, and the sunsets lay crimson on the bosom of the snows. Then came the creeping warmth and the blessing of the spring, and the sick woman revived, as did the flowers where the sunshine made glory on the springing grass.

Madeleine Botta rose from her rock bed almost as hale as ever, and her voice had scarcely lost anything of its fulness when she sang that evening hymn, the 'Psalm of Strong Confidence.'

But Rénée, as the light grew longer and the sweet benediction of the year stole over the frost-held earth, as the swollen streams leapt laughing down amongst the flowers, and the song-birds called in music one to the other, Rénée grew silent and sad.

Life would be easier now. Her mother was in no danger of death or suffering. There would be little to do up there in their cliff cave. Little to do but to wait.

Ah, and the waiting time is the hardest time to such hearts as that of Rénée Janavel.

CHAPTER VI.

GASPARD BOTTA was not one to be easily baffled or beaten; he was young, with muscles of iron and thews as of steel, and he had, moreover, the caution and resource of a hunter, the endurance and the keen eyesight of a mountaineer.

His faith was the faith of his fathers, and for it he would die, readily, unshrinkingly, as his fathers died in the terrible days of the past, and as he had himself seen his countrymen die here, in every hamlet, and by every hearth and home.

But of the actual love of God he knew but very little.

He had meant to do his duty. He had prayed a soldier's prayers, and he had trusted that help Divine would come to him, as it had done to others; to such men as Janavel, and Laurene, and Jayer, men who had gloriously fought in defence of the valleys, and whose names would live while Vaudois hearts yet beat.

But some glimpse of a faith better than this came to him as he left his mother and Rénée in the cave that day.

He could not have put the feeling into words; he scarcely knew when or why, but as he took his lonely way towards the mountains of Angrogna, a sense of God's presence came over him—a searching, demanding presence— a power and a gentleness that asked, not only for his life, but also for his love.

There was the hoarse note of pain ringing through the valleys, the boundless pain of desolation and distress. Why, then, should such thoughts come to him, one of those smitten ones who had suffered, and who yet must suffer? Gentleness—love? surely here on the south slopes of the Alps there was in those terrible years more evidence of the outpouring of God's wrath!

But into the young man's soul there stole some glimpse of the Light that shineth in darkness, of the Love that is behind all wrath, of the Joy that is greater than pain. Not suddenly, but softly and sweetly, even as the spring- time comes upon the coldness and dumbness of the winter-world. He was only a herdsman's son, and his carpentering trade had left him little leisure even for such poor scholarly lore as penetrated to the valleys, but he had heard of One who had also been an outcast, hunted, and done to death; of One whose days were days of suffering, and whose nights were spent in lonely watchings beneath the stars.

And the remembrance of that One came to him now in his own lonely vigil. The Master who had wandered on the Syrian hills, who had stood silent before murderous men; and in heaven, from the great white height of His glorious throne, He yet feels for His brethren who, through great tribulation, are pressing to His feet.

Gaspard understood things better now. There *was* love, and there was gentleness, in spite of the sharpness of that cry of human pain. And Gaspard knelt mute upon the hill-side, with a look upon his face that had never before rested there, a look too full of love for fear, and yet which was too near to awe to take the semblance of gladness.

It seemed to him as though he knelt with his whole soul bare before the glance of God.

The days that followed were full of excitement, anxiety, and trouble. His father had been taken to Luserna, together with all the rest of the valley folk, and there Gaspard followed. It was rather like a lamb searching the den of a wolf, this going into the very stronghold of the Papists; but Gaspard had no thought of evading the duke's troops now. His first duty was to find his father, to tend him, if so it might be; and to carry to him the news of the safety of those two women—news which would go far, so Gaspard guessed, to calm the fever left by that Savoyard lance-thrust.

It was easy to find a way to the interior of the prison, for Gaspard had only to declare that he too was a Vaudois when he was seized and flung into the fortress already full to overflowing with his wretched countrymen; and amongst that pitiful host was his father.

The horrors of that imprisonment will never be fully known now. An old writer says that the Vaudois perished by hundreds of hunger, thirst, and the festering of neglected wounds. Their bread was rough and filled with rubbish, their water was impure and insufficient. The places of the dead—numbers dying every day—were filled with fresh prisoners; the intense heat of summer, the throng of sick and suffering ones, and the crowded state of every corner of the dungeons, made a mass of evil too horrible for recital.

Was not this harder to be borne than were the savage swords of the soldiery, than the fighting at the barricades, than even the brutal insults of victorious foes? For in the past there had at least been the clear air of heaven, and the heart-stirring of struggle; now there seemed only the blankness of noisome despair.

What was it that Henri Botta's parched lips were murmuring as he lay in uneasy sleep across Gaspard's knees? The young man bent to listen, and the broken words he caught were of peace and of beauty, of rest for the weary ones, of the waters of comfort, and the loving-kindness of God.

The old herdsman's rugged nature had also found some trace of gentleness and love amid all this chaos of dismay.

'It must be that the Lord Himself is pitiful,' thought Gaspard, 'and He Himself sends comfort to such as are sore stricken.'

Over and over again did that thought return as he watched frail women rise triumphant above the power of pain, and men—just the rude and untaught peasants of the hills—meeting insult with dignity, and outrage with a smile.

'Be of good cheer, my children,' said one, an aged pastor from Angrogna, 'our Master bore shame and death for our sakes, and shall we shrink from sharing the glory of His cross? Rather thank Him that such as we, the simple valley-folk, are reckoned worthy to follow where He trod!'

They counted twelve thousand captives that were held in the vile durance of the gaols; if it were so, death had opened the prison gates to hundreds upon hundreds of the suffering souls, for it was but three or four thousand men, women, and children whom the Duke of Savoy at last set free. Did he call it 'freedom'?

They were free to leave Piedmont, to take their wretched lives and their precious faith to other lands, but they were not free to return to the valleys. Homeless exiles, ruined wanderers, they might go north or south, east or west; but their homes on the hill-sides should know them no more.

CHAPTER VII.

THE autumn had come, the snow already whitened the Alpine passes; soon the glittering mantle would lie thick on all the hills, and the whirling winds would form deep drifts, and the avalanches come thundering down, and the passage of the Alps would be dangerous exceedingly.

But the order came, imperious, unevadable—the Vaudois were to go.

They would rather trust themselves to their own mountains, to the ice and snow, than stay in those fated prisons; but disease had enfeebled them, imprisonment and bad air had poisoned those whom death had spared. It was a woeful company that set out upon that long and dangerous road.

One of their own historians[A] writes thus of that terrible journey:—

[A] Monastier. Translated from the French.

'The Vaudois travelled in companies, escorted by the soldiers of the duke. They had been promised clothing, but only a small number of jackets and socks were served out to them. It was five o'clock

EXILED.

in the afternoon, at Christmas-tide, when their liberation was announced, with the addition that if they did not set out forthwith it would be out of their power to leave at all, for the order was to be revoked next day. Fearful of losing the chance of liberty, these unfortunate persons, wasted by sickness, set out on their march that very night. There were old men amongst them, worn down by sufferings as well as by years, besides women and children of the tenderest age. That night they marched three or four leagues through the snow, in the most intense frost.'

This first march cost the lives of a hundred and fifty of them. Was it wonderful that these died?

A few days later on at Novalèse, at the foot of Mount Cenis, a troop of the prisoners noticed that a storm was rising on the mountain; they knew well what mountain snow-storms were, and they begged the officer who was in charge to let them stay at Novalèse for a while, out of pity for the weak that were to be found in their ranks. If their request caused delay, they said, they would not ask for food; there was less danger in going without food than in travelling in the face of the storm. The officer refused. The company was forced to proceed on its march, and eighty-six sank in the drifted snow; they were the aged, the worn out, women, and some little children. The bands that followed days after saw the bodies lying frozen on the snow, the mothers still pressing their children in their arms.

Henri Botta would never have survived that journey of toil and horror, had his son Gaspard's arm been less strong and his heart less brave.

Gaspard devoted himself to his father with the whole force of his silent nature; it seemed as though his love for Rénée, pent up and baffled as it was, sought an outlet in this older, less selfish love, and touched it with an enthusiasm which was glorious to behold.

No fatigue seemed to weary the young elastic frame, no privation had power to damp the calm courage which was always ready to cheer and brighten the dark hours of trial.

He had made friends with one of the guards, a soldier whose people he had known in Turin, and from him he managed to get now and then an extra bit of bread, a blanket, and some handfuls of roasted chestnuts—poor and pitiful provision for such a weary way, but to Henri Botta it made, perhaps, the difference between life and death.

Down the steep hill-passes the Vaudois came, troops of gaunt and toil- worn men, large-eyed, weary women, and children who had already learnt the lesson, so strange for childhood—to suffer and be silent. Down on the shores of the Geneva lake, where the winter sun was shining on the ripples until they flashed again like liquid diamonds. Along the ancient roads where many an army had passed before them, but never one so disconsolate and poor; and up to the gates of the town, whence the citizens came hurrying with eager welcome.

They were generous in their kindness, these people of Geneva. Not only welcoming words, but help, food, rest, comfort were freely given to the outcast children of the Alps. Company after company came winding down the mountain sides, but instead of being frightened at such claims upon their charity, the Swiss contended among themselves for the honour of aiding these, their persecuted brethren.

Once more we translate from the Vaudois historian, for the simple statement is more eloquent than modern words can be:—

'Two thousand six hundred Vaudois were received within the walls of Geneva, the feeble remnant of a population of from fourteen to sixteen thousand. Moreover, they were either sick or worn out with fatigue and anxiety, and but ill protected from the rigours of winter by the old garments they had worn in prison. Some there were whose lives ended the very moment their liberty began; these expired between the two gates of the city, too weak to bear the strange sense of joy. But in proportion as the wounds to be dressed were deep, the loving-kindness of the Genevese rose high. They contended with one another who should take home the most destitute; if the invalids and sufferers had any difficulty in walking, men carried them in their arms into their houses. The heavy charge to the state and the people was cheerfully accepted. From the time they had heard of the cruelty of Louis XIV., and of the edicts of the Duke of Savoy, the Swiss had been preparing to offer aid; and when they knew that the Vaudois were to be exiled, and coming to Switzerland, these preparations were redoubled. Five thousand ells of linen were made into garments, and an equal quantity of the woollen stuffs of Oberland. Hundreds of pairs of shoes were laid up in depots. The different cantons distributed the refugees amongst them in a fixed proportion, and the liberality and compassion knew no bounds.'

There was a letter written in July, 1688, signed in the name of the Vaudois by Daniel Forneron and Jean Jalla, a letter yet existing in the archives of Berne. 'We have no language strong enough,' it runs, 'to express our gratitude for your favours; our hearts, penetrated with all your acts of kindness, will publish in distant parts the unbounded charity with which you have refreshed us and supplied all our need. We shall take care to inform our children and our children's children, that all our posterity may know, that, next to God, whose tender mercies have preserved us from being entirely consumed, we are indebted to you alone for life and liberty.'

...　　...　　.　　.

In Geneva, in the early days of 1688, there were aching hearts as well as those that were joyous and thankful. It was delightful to be at rest, to see the sun rise and set, to feel the pure air, and to wander free beneath God's sky. It was strangely sweet to meet together in the churches to sing the praises of the God who had helped and delivered, to hear His Word read in the tongue the people could understand, and know that at last they might worship Him without fear or hindrance.

But the pain that mingled with the gladness was very sharp.

Husbands searched through each arriving company for the wives they had been parted from in the days of the fighting in the valleys. Mothers sought for their sons with hopes that grew fainter with each day that brought refugees, indeed, but not the familiar faces they longed to see. Parents sorrowed for their little ones who had been torn from them and handed over to the Romish convents and schools—the children would grow up to despise them and their religion, and in the coming time, these, who were flesh of their flesh, would be ranked with their enemies.

And how many lay dead, away there beyond the white peaks rising like a giant's rampart against the eastern sky! Dead, in the nameless prison-graves or beneath the winding-sheet of the Alpine snows.

CHAPTER VIII.

IN a Geneva street, where the steep red roofs almost met across the way, in a tall house with a silversmith's sign swinging above the door, lived a Vaudois who had been exiled years ago—the hero of Rora, Joshua Janavel.

The coming of his countrymen stirred him as a trumpet-note might stir an old war-horse. He could only see the glory of their trial, the martyr's crown given to so many, the noble endurance, the faithfulness and steadfastness of heart which they had shown. For him to rejoice at tribulation was no new thing, and he now stood so near to the kingdom of God that he realised more than ever how small are the 'sufferings of this present time' when compared with the glory that shall be revealed.

His aged eyes flashed as he heard of weak women standing firm in face of death and danger; and something of his old ardour awoke again as they reckoned up the names of those who had fallen in a cause so holy, in defending rights so sacred. Once only did his head droop and his voice sink tremulous with feeling, and that was when Henri Botta came to tell him of his grand-daughter Rénée.

He had never seen her, this child of his best-beloved son; he had been driven from the valleys when she was an infant. But he was strangely moved when they told him of her sweetness, her womanly ways and words, of the help she had been to Madeleine, and of how she had faced the trial-storm along with the best and bravest.

'Our God has demanded much from me,' he said in his thin, quavering tones. 'And He knows I have reckoned it as honour to spend and be spent in His cause. I am glad, aye, doubly glad, that the girl, the last of my race, has been ready to take up the standard of Christ, since my weak hands can grasp it no more.'

Henri Botta stood in the doorway, looking down on the old man's face, and he silently thought that neither age nor death would quite rob the Vaudois of Joshua Janavel; such names and memories as his linger long in the hearts of men, and being dead, yet speak in those voices which have far echoings.

The time passed slowly on, the spring, the hot summer, and the scented autumn. There was a great deal stirring in the courts of Europe, but the people of the Cantons were busy with their own affairs, and troubled themselves but little with the rebellion in England, or the war which the Emperor Leopold was bent on waging with France. The fate of the Vaudois concerned them far more nearly.

It was only kindness, and the most active Christian charity, that moved them to make plans for the welfare of the exiles; but the proposals brought forward filled the Vaudois with dismay.

It was suggested that some should be settled in Brandenburg, the dominions of the Great Elector, on the banks of the Elbe; a country which seemed far and foreign to the simple mountaineers. But Brandenburg, distant as it was, was as nothing to the journeys which others urged. The Cape of Good Hope, the unexplored lands of America, these were mentioned as possible homes for the children of the valleys: and the Swiss were inclined to be impatient when they saw how very unwelcome such suggestions were.

The plain fact was that the Vaudois were breaking their hearts with longings for home. Every time they looked to the eastward they saw the Alps gleaming white against the sky; the rushing of the Rhone River was always in their ears, the water which had melted from those upper snows—the snows of the hills.

Here in the west there might indeed be freedom, friends, and no shadow of fear nor pressure of want—but over there, beyond those great white barriers, lay the land they loved, the ruined hearths for which they had shed their blood, the fields their ancestors had tilled, the chestnuts, and the vines, and the mulberries that their grandsires had planted, the graves of their dear ones, the sacred spots made holy by their tears.

The Jews of old sighed by the waters of Babylon over their silent harps: and these poor exiles turned their yearning eyes eastward, unable to forget their Jerusalem, the land of their inheritance.

To Gaspard Botta in these days the hope of return was the very mainspring of life. He worked for his living, as did all the Vaudois; he indeed worked doubly hard, doing his father's share as well as his own, for the old man's strength had never recovered that wound given on the slope of La Vachère, and it was as much as Gaspard could do to keep him from fretting over his uncompleted tasks.

But all the work, hard and anxious as it was, could not entirely blunt the pain which lay for him behind all other things, as shadows lie about the clouds. He could not forget that Rénée was still in danger; that whilst he had shelter, food, comfort, liberty, she and his mother were probably yet hiding among the mountains with but little more shelter and sustenance than God gives to the ravens.

There had been just a chance that they too had been driven off to exile with the rest, and Gaspard had searched with mingled hope and dread through every group of forlorn ones arriving in Geneva. But those he loved were not there. There was no news of them either; they had not been amongst those who had died in prison, nor amongst those who had perished on the journey.

If they were still in life they were near Rora, waiting and watching, as Gaspard knew, with weary hearts and sinking hopes for his coming back to them. His white teeth ground themselves together as he thought of it, and his eyes were dim with a mist of tears as he turned them towards the hills. Was it right to stay quietly here in Switzerland, to let his hands peaceably handle saws and planes? Was it right to let the long days pass in peacefulness when his nearest and dearest needed help so sorely?

He could scarcely hold himself back as he looked at the hills. Surely, his faithful heart kept saying, surely he could reach them, surely he could die with them, if the worst must come.

Not Gaspard only, but the whole company of the banished felt bitter longings and heart-sick yearnings drawing them towards Piedmont, as the magnet draws the steel. Their devotedness, strengthened as it had been by centuries of persecution, nourished their patriotism; they had suffered much for the love of God—they reckoned it now but a small thing to suffer for love of their country.

As the days crept on the longing grew. It was not that they were ungrateful; it was not that they did not prize the calm that had succeeded the struggle, the liberty that had come after the bitter oppression—but their simple hearts just drooped and pined for the valleys.

They had watered that land with their tears and with their blood. No other country could be 'home' to them. They must return, and lift again—if such were God's good will—the voice of praise and prayer from the glens and the hills which now lay desolate.

Men with the same anxiety in their hearts as Gaspard had might be reckoned by the score. There was scarcely a Vaudois who would not have willingly died rather than have surrendered the hope of getting home to the valleys, somehow, some day.

JANAVEL AND THE EXILES IN GENEVA.

In the silversmith's house in the dark Geneva street, groups gathered evening after evening to talk with Janavel. He was, as was natural, a sort of rallying-point for his countrymen. His elbow-chair was the centre of elaborate plannings, fluctuating hopes and fears, and audacious ideas. Here differing ways and means were discussed endlessly; here all men spoke their minds.

And Janavel, who himself could never again strike a blow for country or for faith, was the most eager and hopeful of all.

'Our land is the Lord's,' he would say; 'and in the Lord's good time it shall be restored to our trust.'

   ...   .

It was in July, 1687, that the first attempt at return was made. Two or three hundred impatient ones gathered at Ouchy, on the shores of the lake, full of ardour and hope. But that enterprise was promptly nipped in the bud. The Swiss had pledged their honour to the Duke of Savoy, and considered themselves responsible for the good behaviour of the Vaudois. They could not allow the exiles to cross the frontier with the avowed intention of regaining their country by force of arms, so the expedition was stopped at its very outsetting, and the two or three hundred men sent back to the places from whence they had gathered themselves. So the first effort, small and ill-advised as it was, came to an untimely end.

On the next occasion things were altered. Events marched quickly in those troublous times. In July, 1687, James II. was on the English throne, a bigoted Papist, whose sympathies were all with the extermination of what he called heresy. And in 1687 Louis of France had ample leisure to listen to all priestly plans for crushing the 'new religion.'

In 1689 William of Orange was King of England, a prince wholly devoted to the cause of Protestantism, and King Louis had his hands full to overflowing with wars against the Germans and the Dutch.

And—a fact more important to them than affairs of foreign kings and potentates—the exiles had found what they had hitherto so sorely lacked—a leader. He was one Henri Arnaud, a simple pastor of the valleys, a man trained in the school of hardship, just one of themselves. But he was, in spite of this, a really great man, one not only like Joshua Janavel, but like that other and far greater Joshua, the Hebrew captain of old; for in his heart burnt the holy fire of God's faith and fear, and on his lips was the old battle-cry of the Hebrews, 'Be strong and of a good courage; be not afraid, neither be thou dismayed, for the Lord thy God is with thee whithersoever thou goest.'

It is said that events shape the characters of men rather than men shape the events. If ever this be true, it was the case with Henri Arnaud. His character was the outcome of that hard struggle for existence that had made the Vaudois what they were. Past years of oppression and blood-shedding had nerved his heart and armed his hand; and the purity of the truth for which he and his had suffered had sunk into his soul as the sun's warmth penetrates the surface of the earth.

The Vaudois were as sheep having no shepherd. That very need was a spur to Arnaud. He stood forth, and with one voice they hailed him as their captain. Reverently, and in God's strength, he accepted the trust.

CHAPTER IX.

Arnaud's first care was to gather up the scattered threads of the Vaudois powers, and to unite them, as far as might be, into one cord—a cord which should be firm enough to hold out against the sharp tension that must come.

He had himself been to Holland to confer with William of Orange, the hope of the Protestant world. To him he had unfolded the Waldenses' darling project, a project that seemed wild and hopeless enough when put into words. But Dutch William's soldierly heart warmed as he listened, and for once he threw his diplomatic caution to the winds, as he said: 'Try it, and may God prosper you! If events that I foresee come straightly off the reel, I may be presently in a position to give you aid, a better position than I have now. Go on! trust in yourselves, and trust in God!'

Arnaud recalled those concluding words many and many a time in the months that followed. It would not be timorous and divided hearts that would win the end they held in view; it must be brotherly trust in one another, devoted trust in their fathers' God, that alone could lift them on victoriously.

It was on the 16th of August, 1689, that the rendezvous was fixed on the wooded shores of the upper lake. The summer foliage was thick upon the forest, dense enough to hide the bands of men who came trooping there from all parts of Switzerland. They had to avoid the eyes not only of enemies, but of friends; the magistrates of Chillon and Aigle and Nyon were all on the watch to stop the passage of the Vaudois, as they had stopped the former attempt; but so quietly did they gather, so carefully did they keep their counsel, that the deep woods sheltered more than nine hundred men before the sun went down that day, and that without any suspicion having been excited amongst the Swiss.

Nine hundred men; a small army to attempt the conquest of the valleys, where the soldiers of Savoy were holding the passes, the bridges, and the forts. Undisciplined and ill-armed they were, without stores or means of transport, and without money. Well they knew the dangers that were before them, the privations and fatigues, the scorching heat of the low-lying lands, the bitter snows of the mountains; but in all that crowd of resolute men there was not one who quailed or shrunk.

'Father,' said Gaspard, standing by the old man's side and watching the rugged face wistfully as he spoke, 'Father, wilt thou not abide here, and let me strike thy blow as well as mine own? This arm is surely strong enough; and the thought of thee here, and my mother and Rénée yonder, will nerve it to double strength. Can it not be so? Wilt thou not return in peace to Geneva?'

Henri Botta shook his head; his words were few at any time, fewest when deeply moved.

'Nay,' he said; 'the sons of the Vaudois are but a remnant now, each hand must do its best. Our cause is just. As Israel of old seized sword and buckler to keep hold of the land the Lord had given, so we will fight for the land where our fathers held high the standard of the truth which is in Christ Jesus, the land which is our rightful heritage.'

Gaspard would have urged his point yet further, but the old man would not hear; and in his heart the son knew how impossible it was that Henri should stay at Geneva, feebly trying in loneliness and longing-heartedness to accomplish the task that should earn his daily sustenance. The worn-out body would flag and utterly fail if he were left behind while the rest marched out to regain, if so it might be, their fatherland. And yet, worn and aged as he was, how was he to battle through the dangers that lay before Arnaud and his band?

The sun set; the sweet summer night was silent and serene; the water lapped the flowering rushes and broke in ripples against the rocky shore; a star or two shone in the gleaming sky, and beyond the far horizon-line the shimmer of moonlight was creeping up the east.

The men stood in groups among the trees, strange thoughts thronging about their hearts—a solemn sense of present peril, and eager longings to take the first step of their great enterprise; but they stood quietly for the most part. Such times as these are not times for talk, and the trouble-trained Vaudois had learned to possess their souls in silence.

It was two hours from midnight; presently a voice broke over the stillness —it was the leader, Arnaud, and his words were words of prayer. Kneeling there in the shadow of the trees, his eyes lifted to that growing eastern radiance, he poured out his pleadings—he asked for Divine help where other help was small and scant; for Divine guidance where a guiding hand would be so sorely needed; for Divine strength to fill the failing hands and brace the feeble knees. 'Thou hast helped our fathers throughout the long ages, O God of our hope! help us still, according to Thine ancient promises. Be favourable to the simple and the needy, and preserve the souls of the poor; that our tongues may talk of Thy righteousness, and the mountains bring peace to Thy people!'

Gaspard heard the deep tones of his father's 'Amen.' The old man's face showed sharp against the gleam of the sky, and upon it was a look that silenced Gaspard's fears. Henri Botta was asking for the strength that is greater than all human powers, the strength that is never denied. One sharp pang shot through Gaspard's heart, and then the bitterness of his anxiety was gone for ever. Failure, death itself might be before them; but he felt, he knew, that God would care for His aged servant, and lift him safely to the shores of that country where the nations shall be healed.

Across the still stretches of the Geneva water, over the sleeping lake into the shadow of the further shores; then, landing on the Savoy side, and marshalling their ranks in such brave battle-front as they could show, these nine hundred men began their march.

Their historian[B] says: 'They were a small company to attack Savoy—a company, on the other hand, far too numerous for the slender means of sustenance to be found in the by-places through which they intended to go; an untrained assemblage formed of persons of every age, hardened, it is true, by toil, but yet strangers to military discipline and manœuvres. What would become of them as they pressed on, forcing their way against an armed resistance, through inhospitable tracts and deep defiles, by the sides of precipices, and over rocks crowned with eternal snow? Now alone on the strand of the lake they have just crossed, they tread on the soil they are about to bathe with their sweat and their blood. No illusion deceives them; the hard reality, with its dangers and privations, is before their eyes, stern as the truth. But no one draws back. The prize of the conflict seems to them worthy of the highest sacrifices; it is a terrestrial home, to the recollection of which they have attached their faith and hope of salvation in Christ Jesus. In setting out, sword in hand, to reconquer it their hearts are at ease, for their cause is just…. They desire to remain under the observation of God, the righteous Judge, and beneath His holy protection. They hope to repeat on their march, and in every encounter, "Jehovah is our Banner." '

[B] Antoine Monastier.

···   ···   ·   ·

The blessed summer-time brought beauty once more to the valleys. The flowers shone again in the deserted gardens, and the garlanded leaves of vines hid the breaches in the shattered walls of Rora.

Madeleine Botta came of sturdy mountain race, and her vigour came again to her with the throbbing, teeming life of the summer world. It was Rénée now whose strength flagged, Rénée whose eyes were lustreless, and whose footsteps were slow.

The months, long weary months, had told on her courage and broken her spirit; it was in the spring of 1687 when the thunderbolt of desolation had fallen on her home, when the house-master and Emile and her own Gaspard

53

had gone out to keep the barricades. It was high summer-time when Gaspard had crept away from their cave shelter, and she had dashed the tears from her eyes, that her vision might hold him, clear and unbedimmed, until he had turned that sharp angle of rock where the broken bridge lay damming up the stream. It was again the summer when Madeleine lay so nigh to death, and she, in lowliness and sore distress, fought with the fever that threatened to rob her of her 'mother.'

And now again it was summer-time. Was the brightness but empty mockery? Was the sunshine to gladden all the world save the homes of the Vaudois, and the heart of Rénée Janavel?

Madeleine watched her in silence. She knew something, and guessed more, of this heart-sickness that weighed upon the girl's elastic nature until her Rénée seemed as limp and nerveless as one of the unpropped vines in yonder ravaged valley. She did not sympathise nor seek by word of counsel to probe or heal the hurt. She waited with the trustful patience that was part of her character until her spoken sympathy could be followed out by help.

Some semblance of peace had come to the country-side; the professors of the 'new religion' had been driven out with sword and with fire: and there must needs be cessation of persecution when none are left to be persecuted. Even such refugees and stragglers as had hidden in the mountains had mostly perished or been seized ere this, and even the priests and preaching friars were content with their finished work, and let their energy in heretic-hunting slacken down.

Madeleine and Rénée ventured occasionally into the empty villages, and walked abroad upon the upper slopes, even by daylight. There were some cottagers dwelling on the foot-road to Casiana, who, although Romanists, were as friendly as they dared to be; and from them Madeleine now and then heard stray scraps of intelligence; she had been kind to them in years gone by, and even the fury of the death-decrees that had desolated the valleys had not quite extinguished their memories of gratitude.

Indeed, during the last winter they had given more than kind words—many a great cake of black-bread, many a bag of chestnuts and handful of barley-meal had found its way to the refuge on the cliff; and when the two women had expostulated they would be told that it was but part of the produce of their own lands, which had been divided amongst the Catholics by the duke. 'And,' the kindly words would finish with, 'and, if you are so very particular, Henri and Gaspard shall pay us for all when they come back again.'

But Rénée shuddered when she heard that: she had hoped for long and long, but now her hope was dead. Neither the house-master nor Gaspard would ever come back!—so she believed, in her dreary despair.

In the long June days Madeleine heard news which made her decide on trying to light again the dead hope in Rénée's heart. Some rumours of what was happening in the great centres of life, in Paris, and Vienna, and Turin, penetrated as far as Luserna, and echoes reached the friendly cottage on the Casina road, and finally were heard by Madeleine.

Savoy was stripped of troops; the duke had need of all his soldiers in Piedmont; the King of France was fighting with the emperor and the Dutch; and the Vaudois were massed in the cantons of Switzerland, looking with longing eyes at the hill-ranges of their native land.

'Child,' said Madeleine, 'once, long months ago, you spoke of creeping away to the Swiss country, to live in security where God has granted freedom to serve Him unchidden. Do you remember, dear? and how I felt I could not face the weary journey, nor bear to see you go alone? And—— '

'Mother!'—the interruption came with a flash of the girl's old spirit —'mother! would it be possible for me to have left you?'

'Dear child! but there is now no question of leaving me—we will go together, Rénée; and it may be we shall find our dear ones yonder; and God's sun shall shine upon my eventide in those blessed lands where there is yet the daylight of His truth.'

BREAD FOR THE WAYFARERS.

CHAPTER X.

Two women walking northward through the quiet air of the summer-time, carrying modest bundles on their shoulders, their arms laden with osier-baskets, which they offered in exchange for a bit of bread or a night's lodging, were not travellers likely to awaken remark or cupidity. Madeleine Botta and her foster-child traversed the Luserna valley unmolested. The hue and cry after the heretics had died away—perhaps even a reaction had set in, and there might be pity mingled with any suspicions that the Papist peasants entertained as the two passed by.

There was a garrison at the town of Luserna, and large monasteries established at La Torre and Bobbio. But these places were easily avoided, the travellers entering only the most retired hamlets and hill-side cottages when seeking a market for their wares, and, unless in want of food, keeping as far as possible from all human haunts. Though immediate danger seemed afar off, they had suffered too bitterly not to be cautious.

The planning and the caution were mostly left to Madeleine, for Rénée still looked round her with indifferent eyes, and seemed too hopeless, too miserable to care whether they ever reached Switzerland or not. She walked by her foster-mother's side, gentle, indeed, and sweet and bidable, but unlike the gay girl whom Gaspard had wooed before the fury of this last persecution had burst upon Savoy.

One evening, it was the 29th of August, the travellers halted on the slopes of the Giuliano Pass. They had come through Armatier, and up the banks of the torrent that runs down to Bobbio from the mighty glacier-skirts of Mount Cournan. They were weary, for the day's march had been unusually long.

They had taken shelter in a cottage—deserted as so many Piedmont cottages were in those sad years—and Madeleine, folding her cloak about her, lay down to rest.

Rénée stood by the doorway; the broken hinges told their tale of forcible entry; the few rude articles of furniture were broken likewise; the feet of the spoiler had entered here, and that not so very long ago, judging from the splinters of the fir-wood which showed white in the gathering shadow.

The girl's eyes were fixed on the snowy dome of the great mountain which shone to the northward in a radiance and purity which might almost befit the hills of heaven, round its feet soft mist, as of opal and of pearl, floated in streaming trails and wreaths. And beyond it the clear sky was fair and stainless in its immensity of blue; one glittering point of sharp silver trembled above—the first shy star of the summer night.

'Rénée,' Madeleine called to her in tones which were full of love—of yearning love that longed to help her child. 'Rénée, of what thinkest thou now in the evening silence? Of the difficult ways we have trodden? or of those we yet must tread? Shall our prayer to our Father this night begin with thankfulness? or with pleading for yet more of His help? Come here to me, Rénée, and let me hear thy voice.'

The girl turned and came to her side. The listless mood had lifted, and there was a sense of surpressed emotion in her gait, in her voice, and her very hands, as she stretched them out to Madeleine.

'Is there ever an answer, mother?' she said.

'An answer?'

'Aye, to these prayers of ours? And to all the sighs and burden of prayer that has gone up from the valleys these centuries past? Does He hear us at all, our God? or are the places of His dominion too wide for Him to have thought to spare for the narrow shelters where the Vaudois have tried to hide from the spoiler and oppressor? Look there, mother! see where the head of that mountain lifts itself into the skies; it is the same, always the same, silent and cold and cruel, though our forefathers were hunted across its ridges in the past years, and we are now creeping wearily towards its feet. It cares nothing. It smiles in the sun or it frowns in the tempest, and heeds not Savoyard, nor Frenchman, nor Vaudois! Mother, is it not like this Power that we implore?— this Power that is deaf to our cries—indifferent, though we His servants are dying here on His earth?'

There was no reply to this outpouring of long pent-up emotion. Madeleine drew the girl's figure close to her side, and laid her forehead against the throbbing breast. A faint wind sighed amongst the pine boughs, and a far-off rustle and dull roll told of the passage of a distant avalanche. Rénée shivered.

'Though He slay me, yet will I trust in Him,' repeated Madeleine, the fervent words coming distinct and brave, although her lips were trembling.

A VISION OF THE MOUNTAINS—'COLD AND CRUEL.'

'It is through suffering that we must follow our Lord,' she went on, after a long pause. 'He refused the kingdoms of this world and the glory of them, and chose to wander homeless, and to die in shame. O child, thou hast lost much, and even yet more may be asked of thee—home and dear ones are gone; food, raiment, life itself may be wrenched away—but, Rénée, do not give up thy faith!—thy faith in the rest that remaineth for the Vaudois—thy faith in thy Saviour, who loveth even thee and me!'

The girl was weeping. Not the burning tears of a passionate despair, but the blessed drops that ease the heart from whence they flow. Into her soul there came some faint fair imagining of the meaning of it all—this trial and torture, this desolation and weariness of waiting. Just such a glimpse as had come to Gaspard when he knelt alone on Mount Vadolin came now to her. Life, and the wreck of such riches as life had held for her, was small indeed compared with this higher weal and wealth—the unsearchable riches of Christ.

And, presently, when the purple shade crept over the gleaming snows of the upper pass, and even the mountain's mighty brow was shadowed—two voices sang the 'Psalm of Strong Confidence,' albeit the notes fell quaveringly, and the words were mingled with the echoes of sobs.

> 'The earth trembled and was still, wher God arose
> To help the meek upon the earth.
> Then the fierceness of man shall be turned to His praise,
> And the fierceness of the violent shall be restrained.'

CHAPTER XI.

T<small>HE</small> Vaudois troops (if the word 'troops' can be applied to the nine hundred followers of Henri Arnaud) crossed Lake Leman on the 18th of August, and at once pressed southwards through La Chablais and Faucigny.

They were already on the enemy's ground, or rather in the dominions of the Duke of Savoy, but their own country lay beyond the huge shoulders of Mont Blanc and Mont Cenis; and they had many weary leagues to win before they could look upon their enterprise as fairly begun. They had no

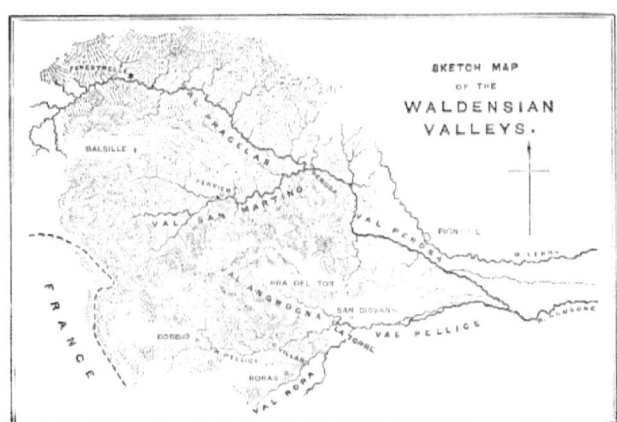

SKETCH MAP OF THE WALDENSIAN VALLEYS.

quarrel with the towns of Upper Savoy; all they asked was free passage, and to be allowed to purchase food—a demand not always granted.

At Boëge they met with the first resistance; and here Arnaud made his first stroke of generalship. He seized several gentlemen as hostages, and made one of them write letters to the mayors of the towns of Vin, St. Joyre, and Cluse, to the effect that the Vaudois 'had requested hostages to accompany them, to give an account of their conduct, which should be in all respects honest and regular; that they wished to pay for everything they demanded, and to go peaceably on their way.' The mayors were advised 'not to sound the tocsin nor to alarm the country, and to withdraw their people, if they were already under arms.'

These letters, signed by all the hostages, names well known and honoured in Savoy, had an excellent effect; and the little army pressed on up the Valley of the Arve, to gain, if possible, the Bridge of Sallenches, before the news of their approach could give opportunity for it to be fortified against them.

Just as they came down the Maglan road, they saw a horseman galloping towards the town to give the alarm. Sallenches being the chief town of Faucigny, there, if anywhere, their passage would be disputed, and it was of the utmost importance to make what speed they might, that the town might be taken unawares.

Within a hundred paces of the great wooden bridge they halted, putting themselves in their best battle-array. A regular army corps might have smiled to see their uneven ranks, their curious collection of weapons, their queer attempts at soldierly equipment. But a second glance at those lines of steadfast faces, a further thought of what those steady eyes, those firm lips, and eager looks must mean, would have put an end to smiling. The nine hundred men drawn up before the Bridge of Sallenches were no fitting mark for scoffing— so much at least was certain. The townsmen hoped to gain time by parleying. They sent deputies and messengers; and meanwhile were getting the guard under arms.

Arnaud divined the meaning of their delay. He looked carefully at the bridge, laden as it was with houses, and flanked by towers which in half-an-hour would be filled with soldiers. He looked along the ranks of his men. *He* could read the meaning of those steadfast faces! The word was given. There was a rush forward. Swift and silent—the mountaineers had crossed the bridge. Sallenches was won.

The passage of Sallenches, rather, for they dared not loiter in the town. They hurried on to Cablau, where, weary and hungry, and soaked with the heavy rain, they laid down to rest. But they raised thankful hearts in gratitude to God that night.

The chronicler of their journey writes: 'These poor people blessed God that they had marched so far successfully, without fighting or loss of men, over bridges and through defiles where a few courageous defenders could have done them irreparable injury, and they were grateful for a peaceful night after so much fatigue and anxiety. Rest was very necessary, for they were about to face difficulties of which the prospect might have shaken the courage of persons quite unfatigued and free from anxiety; how much more men who for a number of days and nights had known no rest or sleep but what they could enjoy during their brief halts, not to mention the mental disquietude which scarcely allowed them to close their eyes! Now they had reached the foot of the most gigantic of the Alps, whose heads are hoary with eternal snows, and whose precipitous sides are scored by a few perilous paths by which no traveller can come without danger. The Vaudois had to traverse the forests of the lower grounds, to clamber rocks surmounted with silver snows, hollowed out with dazzling glaciers and torrent waterfalls; they came not into this sublime scenery to admire the works of God, but to shun men and cities, to breathe free air—as did the chamois bounding on the heights above them, or the eagle that soared over their heads. They had to cross numerous spurs and ranges of the hills, lateral branches of the principal chain; to do this it was necessary to climb from the bottom of one valley, only to descend again into the next. Often they could find nothing to maintain them but milk and cheese and the frozen water of the mountains. The rain frequently beat upon their backs, bent with fatigue; and their suffering feet slipped upon the stones and in the stony ravines. Late at night they would perhaps reach shepherds' huts, barren and cold, where they would make fires by unroofing the hovels for fuel; a plan that warmed them indeed, but exposed them to the fury of the elements. And this was their daily experience for eight days. But Arnaud, the zealous and renowned leader of the little troop, restored, by his holy and excellent exhortations, the courage of those who followed him. He spared himself least of all. His foot took the most difficult path, his platter was the last to be filled. And in the morning and at the night-falling he, in the name of his little flock, asked for them the strength and confidence of God.'

Such were the first steps of the 'Glorious Return.'

CHAPTER XII.

THE Vaudois had lived from generation to generation a life described by a modern writer as one of absolute seclusion, 'without thought or forethought of foreign help or parsimonious store;' drinking draughts from their own grape-clusters and saving of last year's harvest only seed enough for the next. They had the serenity given them by God and by Nature, with thanks for the good and submission for the evil; they persisted through better and worse in their fathers' ways, in the use of their fathers' tools, and in holding to their fathers' fields as faithfully as the trees to their roots or the lichens to their rocks.

It was this simplicity, this serenity, and persistency, that carried them forward now. A regular army would have been hampered by a hundred needs and cares and strategies. Arnaud and his men went from Nyon to Sallenches, from Mont Blanc to Mont Cenis, from the Arve to the Doire, stepping forward with the confidence of children and the 'foolishness' of the saints.

Some opposition they had already overcome. They avoided the French garrison of Exilles, but they could not avoid the Marquis de Larrey, who with two thousand five hundred soldiers kept the passage of the Doire at Salabertrand.

They had hurried past Exilles, hoping to win this bridge as they had won the bridge over the Arve, but the night was falling as they came within sight of the place, and they were forced to halt at a village to snatch rest and a meal. They asked if they could buy bread. The answer, significantly spoken, sounded threatening.

'Come on to the river, you will get there all you want; they are preparing excellent suppers for you.'

It was Gaspard Botta to whom those words were said, and he reported them at once to Arnaud. The chief shared his fears as to what they might mean, but there was no room for hesitation in Arnaud's heart. He gathered his men for the usual evening prayer; perhaps his words were more intensely fervent, higher in their note of faith than they had been before, and the 'Amen' that rose from the tightened bearded lips was fit echo to such petitions.

The darkness was lying on the world unbroken by moon or star; only the snow-gleam and the pale line below the western clouds gave light enough to see the strongly-rushing river, white here and there with broken water, and the dark span of the wooden arches stemming the torrent.

The tramp of their feet provoked the sharp challenge—

'Who goes there?'

'Friends,' cried Arnaud; 'all we ask is——'

But the answer came in a tempest of bullets, and wild cries of 'Kill! kill!' The mountaineers flung themselves on their faces, and the deadly hail flew almost harmless above their heads. Then when the French muskets were empty Arnaud dashed on.

'Courage,' he called. 'Forward, Vaudois! the bridge is won!'

And it was even so! The fierce onslaught of the desperate men confused and shattered the enemy's lines. Ten or twelve wounded, fourteen or fifteen killed, was the Vaudois loss—and their gain was the passage of the Doire, the open door to their valleys!

The French had fled. The town was at the mercy of its captors. They seized what military stores they needed, and blew up what ammunition they could not carry away. They did sup well that night; the threat had turned to a prophecy.

The next day they reached the summit of the mountain of Sci. It is a high crest overlooking the Valley of Clusone, fearful enough when howling with the gales of winter and dark with the shadow of snow-clouds; but to-day the sun bathed it in warm light, and the sky shone over it, fair as a shield of silver. Arnaud halted his army there on the brow, and silently pointed to the scene before them.

There were the well-known landmarks; there the sharp horizon-line of their own mountains, the hills of their native land. Before their eyes it lay, bright in the sunshine, the country of the Vaudois—the home for which they had hungered—the land for which they had longed. The very wind as it blew from off it seemed charged as with breath of blessing.

They knelt reverently, with one accord, lifting moist eyes to the blue sky-depths, while Arnaud, their captain and their minister, poured out thanksgiving and praise for the help that had brought them thus far. 'The Lord hath done great things for us, whereof we are glad. Turn again our captivity, O Lord, that they that sow in tears may reap in joy. Though we walk in the midst of trouble, Thou wilt revive us. Thou shalt stretch forth Thine hand against the wrath of our enemies, and Thy right hand shall save us.'

Those Hebrew psalms came to their lips in the day of toil and suffering, and they come still to all Christian souls, fitting all needs, singing as they do of human sins and failures, of Divine forgiveness, and God's triumphant glory; they stir the innermost hearts of men as they echo down through the ages, as true and real now as when first sung by the sweet singers of Israel.

Each day increased the difficulties gathering about the devoted band. The news of their approach had reached Piedmont, and troops were on the alert to intercept their march. The valleys were not to be gained without a deadly struggle; and Arnaud knew it.

Eleven days after leaving Geneva they set foot in the first Vaudois village, Balsille, in the Vale of St. Martino. It was empty; the new inhabitants had fled down the river-bank towards Le Perrier, where a strong force of Piedmontese soldiers were forming across the valley.

But the Vaudois avoided the force they could scarcely hope to defeat. Arnaud turned to the south-westward, up the gorge of Prali, intending to reach the Valley of Luserna by the Guliano Pass, leaving Le Perrier and its garrison on his left.

There was utter peace up this mountain valley, the peace of the great hills in the warmth and hush of the summer. The church—the 'Temple of Prals, as they had used to call it—was still standing; it had been transformed into a place for Romish worship, but the white walls raised by Vaudois hands were there, and the roof-tree that had echoed to the people's prayers for generations.

Henri Botta bared his head as he entered it. He gave small heed to the movements and exclamations of his comrades, who were sternly removing all superstitious ornaments and popish adornments; his heart had gone back to the old days when he had come here from Rora to woo Madeleine, who had lived in yonder farm-stead all her girlish years—one could see it yet, the broken gable rising sharp above the tufted chestnut grove; and there in that humble cottage by the foot-bridge, the heroic pastor Leydat had lived— Leydat, who had been martyred in 1686, seized while singing psalms with his hunted flock in a cave below the mighty crest of Mont Cournan. Henri Botta almost thought he could yet hear his well-known voice as he read from the great Bible chained on the desk by the further arch; a voice easily to be held in memory, with its deep cadences and rolling utterance.

Leydat was dead—blessedly dead among God's saints in God's keeping; the farm-stead was wrecked; the great Bible and its clasps torn away—and Madeleine—who could say what had befallen her since they parted at the entrenchments across the Rora Valley? How long ago it seemed!

THE CHAINED BIBLE.

And the house-master held his own withered hand before his eyes, gazing at it curiously, evidence as it was of his age and infirmity. Such a shaking, knotted, feeble old hand! A marvel, is it not, that one so aged and broken as he should have managed to live through the days of their daring march hence from Switzerland?

'God has been my helper,' he murmured. 'He, and His gift to me, my boy Gaspard.'

CHAPTER XIII.

Bᴏᴛᴛᴀ could see Gaspard from where he stood, and his eyes kindled and grew luminous as he watched the athletic figure bending under its load of forage. The young carpenter had proved himself good metal, and Arnaud— one of whose many gifts it was to judge men's qualities swiftly and justly— had advanced him from the ranks to a place of trust about his own person. There was not a man in his whole troop that he trusted more fully than Botta's son, Gaspard.

'This was your mother's home,' said the house-master, later that evening, when he and Gaspard had withdrawn themselves a little from the rest, and climbed the steep bank which swept up from the hill-torrent to the bastion of rock that kept watch and ward above. 'Your mother's home. Here I saw her first, binding rye in those fields—the grey and silver rye. I never see it now but I think of that day in autumn, two and thirty years ago. Two and thirty years— a long time, Gaspard, to you, for it is more than your whole life; but to me it seems but a handful of days, few and evil, like those of Jacob. Two and thirty years!'

'There are other measurements than hours and weeks,' returned the young man slowly; 'I have learned that. How long is it since we crossed the mountains into Switzerland? They count our exile as a score or two of months, to me it is a very lifetime.'

'His day is as a thousand years, and a thousand years in His sight but as a day,' returned Henri Botta, whose slower mind had not grasped the inner meaning of his son's words.

'And,' Gaspard went on, 'there are the small things we give our lives to grasp, and the great things we have not eyes to see. Will God judge us for our foolishness, and punish us for our blindness in the day of the account?'

'He bids us ask for wisdom, Gaspard, and He has promised us the light.'

Still he did not follow the workings of his son's mind, but he added:

'God understandeth our frame, and remembereth that we are but dust. If His heaven is high and far above us, His Son came here that in all things *He* might understand.'

The young man did not answer. He was thinking of that day on the Angrogna hill when first he caught an inkling of the truth that the life is more than meat, and the body than raiment—that day when it was first given him to see that God's stroke, falling as sharp pain, is yet His Hand of Love.

It was but little that they seemed able to effect, this handful of men marching across the confines of their native land; their bivouac fires were few and feeble on that summer night in the Prali fields; and Henri Botta's white hairs and Gaspard's ill-armed hands showed as poor samples of the stuff of which Arnaud's army was made. Yet, judged by wider measurements, they were not ignoble, nor was their effort mean. These men of the Vaudois were holding forth to the world the spectacle of reverent faith in the promises of their God. They trusted in Him, and they believed that that fervent trust would never be confounded.

As the notes of Madeleine's evening psalm died down on the hill-side, a figure raised itself from behind a jutting crag and crept stealthily off in the darkness. The two women, well used to the desolate mountains, slept serene and safe in the hut. Rénée's head rested on her foster-mother's arm, and over the sweet flower-like face there was spread the reflection of the peace that passeth understanding. The evil mood that had tried her faith was gone, and in its place had come the nameless Light that shines from the Spirit of Comfort. She was dreaming, not of Gaspard, nor of happy days past or come, but of her Mother-Madeleine and her 'Psalm of Confidence.'

Yet all about that ruined hut were cruel and violent men, the hired soldiery of the duke. Men little better than brigands, who had been sent expressly upon work of rapine and slaughter, that a 'strong hand' might crush the Vaudois now and for ever.

The singing had roused the attention of the outpost of the troops that had been thrown forward to keep the Giuliano Pass. A soldier had crept forward to reconnoitre the advance of Arnaud, and his men had made the Savoyards cautious, and the sound of a Huguenot hymn might mean serious mischief. But the alarm died away in a brutal scoff, when the scout brought news that it was no meeting of heretics, no vanguard of the Vaudois army, but an aged woman and a young girl singing themselves to sleep under the shattered roof of a herdsman's hut.

'Leave them in peace,' ordered the captain, an old soldier, who was weary from his forced march, and who wished for undisturbed repose. 'If those two hundred hounds of mine start such a quarry, there will be no quiet for hours. So hold thy tongue an thou canst, Antoine, and go back to thy post. Dost hear? It is well.'

But when the sun had climbed the morning sky, and the scented tassels of the pines were swaying to the breeze stealing from the snow-fields, when the soldiers had shaken off their slumbers and were clamouring for their morning meal, they might do what they pleased with such trifles as a couple of defenceless women, for all their captain cared.

There were, as he said, but two hundred of them; but half that number might hold the Giuliano Pass; the Vaudois were marching southwards by Rodoret and Prali, as the duke's troops were all aware. What mattered it? Arnaud and his horde of fanatics might beat themselves to pieces against the swords of the soldiers without risk or loss to that two hundred, so wonderfully did the rocks stand round the forge, an entrenchment and barrier stronger than mortal hands could build, a fastness which neither Arnaud nor his mountaineers could force.

The captain laughed as he glanced up at the cliffs towering towards the snows. Ah, yes! it would be strange indeed if his two hundred could not hold the Giuliano Pass against greater odds than Arnaud was likely to bring.

When at peep of day rude hands flung open the hut door, and ruder voices called across the empty space, there fell a brief silence of surprise upon the group of men. The hut was vacant: the quarry had fled.

THE HUT WAS VACANT.

Whither? Who could tell? As well hunt for the proverbial needle amongst a bundle of hay as seek two women of the valleys amongst their native wilds. They might carry news to Arnaud—true, but Arnaud might have the news and welcome! He was not likely to profit much by it.

So the soldiers hung their camp-kettles over their fires and pushed chestnuts into the edges of the ashes and made ready their morning meal, blythe as the birds in the copse of birches below them. And yonder where the mighty mountains sloped northward and eastward towards Prali, Madeleine and her foster-child sped through the forest paths with pale looks and quickened breathings. They had lived through so much, escaped so much, but perhaps the fiercest danger was this last—the Savoy guard on the Giuliano Pass.

Madeleine's quick ear had caught the sound of voices, and a very little investigation had shown her the nest of hornets amidst which she and Rénée had lain down to rest. They were well used to see danger staring them in the face, but even Madeleine's heart grew sick with fear as they threaded the stony ways in that gleaming midsummer dawn. A false step might betray them, and how have cool caution sufficient to plant each step silently down those difficult paths?

CHAPTER XIV.

ONCE clear of the defile, with its perils, the two women hurried onwards, each turn of the hills revealing some well-remembered scene to Madeleine. There, below, was Prali, where she had lived when a girl; those tall poplars by the waters seemed to be unchanged since the days when she had driven her cows into their shadow; and there away to the right was the gleam of water where the thirteen lakes lay in the snowy mountain spurs like dew-drops in the bosom of a rose; and surely no rose could be lovelier than was the snow at that moment, as the sun broke through the level mists that veiled his dawning.

'It was my father's home, Rénée,' the woman murmured wistfully, 'my home, where I played with my brothers, where I sat spinning at my mother's side, where Henri Botta came and taught me how to love him. Long ago—ah, yes, so long ago! There is the church, look, Rénée; there was a bell in the wooden tower that used to ring for prayer. The papists say often that we Vaudois do not pray; had they lived in Prali they had learned better things of us. Rénée, child, tell me canst thou see the tower? thine eyes are clearer than mine, canst thou see it, the little red tower with its painted bell-cage? It was Henri, my brave Henri, that reared it, it was that building-task that brought him to Prali. Ah, how long ago!'

'And I shall never see him on earth again!' she went on more to herself than to Rénée.

'I shall never hear his voice, as when evening brought him home to me at Prali and at Rora; but he is in higher hands than ours, ah, yes. And I know that in the land of light I shall see him and hear him, when these turmoils and troubles are past. Only a little while more, a very short while, and our Master will call me too.'

'It must not be that I am left behind,' said Rénée, with a girl's swift thought of self. 'Thou art all I have, mother, and we must die together.'

The woman turned slowly from regarding the distance, and let her eyes rest upon the sweet sad face so near her own. 'That is as the Master wills,' she answered softly. 'He loves thee better than I do.'

'Yes,' answered Rénée, a smile breaking over the sorrow of her mouth. 'Yes, I know it now.'

It was true; in the thick darkness the Day-star had arisen for her, the faint and far-off glimmer of God's great light of truth. Earthly trial and torture bites sharply, and such griefs as had beaten on Rénée Janavel and on her people may well demand human courage and break human hearts; but the truth was true for them, as it is true for all time, that God's love is stronger than pain, that in the midst of sorrow His comfort can be sweet, and that even 'men's fierceness shall turn to His praise.'

They were far from the crest of the Giuliano Pass by this time, and they could hear no sign of pursuit. They turned aside to rest awhile on a grassy slope which broke the hill-side with its long terrace, a lovely stretch of sward, where flowers gleamed amongst the grass, and the bees were flying heavily above the patches of wild-thyme. The shadow of a birch-tree crossed it, making a trembling play of light and shade in the strong sunshine; and below this clear space of grass and flowers there came a tossed and tangled brake, full of creeping plants and broken stones, and tussocks of moss, and the stately spires of some alpine larkspur crowded thick with bloom.

Here they sat, silent for the most part, for their hearts were too full for much speech, but between them lay a sacred sympathy that scarcely needed words.

Madeleine's yearning eyes were still seeking out familiar landmarks, her memory was busy with the past; but her fingers were closed tightly over her foster-child's hand, and the sense of Rénée's presence lay in the background of her thoughts as the blue sky lay behind those birchen boughs. And the girl's head drooped and her eyes were downcast, but her soul was steady and stilled. God's ways might be mysterious and His lessons hard, but the ways and the lessons were those of her Father, and she could trust His love.

Then, suddenly, over the peace and the stillness there fell a horror of alarm.

Down below them, coming by the poplar rows and the river-bank, were armed men. They could see the regular ranks, and catch the gleam of steel. *Soldiers!* And to these hunted women of the valleys that word meant terror and the danger of death.

Should they hide themselves amongst the stones and trees? Should they fly to the right or left?

'Ah,' Rénée's hand clutched her mother's convulsively as the cry left her lips, 'they are all about us; see!'

Dark forms were climbing the hill-side on either hand. Below them was that marching troop. Behind them was the guard of the Giuliano Pass. Was there then any hope in flight?

They shrank back into the shadow of the birch, a flickering and slight shadow at best, but any movement might betray them if they crossed the bare slope; sunlight so strong as that which bathed the grass would reveal them only too sharply. Madeleine hid her face in her hands, and lifted her heart in prayer. Renée watched the approaching figures with wide-open defiant eyes, her beautiful head held back like a stag at bay; she threw her black cloak over the white coif and kerchief of her foster-mother, and flung her own scarlet capucin into the shadow; it came naturally to her to protect her mother— Madeleine, but even as she covered and sheltered her the thought came flashing through her brain that it was now for the last time. Surely the end had come.

There could be no escape. The troops were advancing rapidly, led by those who apparently knew every feature of the ground. The scouts were close upon them now, the sound of their feet crashing through the underwood could be distinctly heard, even the hoarse tones of their voices and the clank of their accoutrements. Madeleine cowered yet lower, and a whispered word of prayer came like a groan from her lips.

And then, starting forwards with a jerk as of a bow released from its tension, Renée snatched her hands from her mother's hold, and held them out with a ringing cry.

'Gaspard!' she called, 'Gaspard!'

The hill above her echoed it, the dear, long-unuttered word; and Madeleine, bewildered, repeated it in her turn, as if speaking in a dream. 'Gaspard! Gaspard!'

And there were hurrying steps bounding over the brake, and a voice loud and strong calling across the distance. And then....

But neither Renée nor Madeleine could remember very clearly what happened then. They knew that, instead of danger, help had come, instead of death a newer and dearer life, instead of the faces of their foes the sight of their best-beloved.

And there on the hill-slopes where he had first beheld her Henri Botta met his wife again. Safe after perils unspeakable; together after bitterest separation. Was it strange that for the moment they forgot that there was still trouble and trial in God's fair world, and that while the golden sunshine lay bright upon the grass they should, for those brief minutes at least, forget that the Vaudois had yet to win the valleys?

'Renée,' whispered Gaspard, holding the girl's hands in both his own, and looking down into her frank eyes as he spoke, 'Renée, I trusted thee to the

'GASPARD!' SHE CALLED, 'GASPARD!'

care of our Father above, and He has preserved thee alive.'

'But I,' and her answering voice sunk and broke, 'but I have been faithless —unworthy. I have doubted. I have despaired.'

The tramp of the main body of Arnaud's army was close upon them. Gaspard remembered his place, which was on the advance guard.

'I must go,' he said hurriedly. 'At our noonday halt I shall find thee. My father and mother and thee—keep together, keep with the troops. Farewell for a short while, dear one; and may God grant us each a braver faith, and then a larger heart of thankfulness!'

CHAPTER XV.

THE two women could give Arnaud very full and important information as to the whereabouts of the enemy. Madeleine, who knew every yard of the ground, could explain just where a passage was possible, exactly where the best hope lay of forcing or outflanking the Savoy guard. In their hurried escape at daybreak they had seen the spot chosen for the defence of the pass, and they could guess at the number of men entrenched behind the giant boulders, and the means they had taken to render the natural defences of the place impregnable.

The Vaudois halted about three or four miles from the crest of the gorge, well on the Prali side, and out of sight of the duke's men. There was not one amongst them all but knew the enormous importance of the next few hours. If they were repulsed and beaten back, the Marquis de Larrey, who was in command of the French troops beyond the Doire, or the Marquis de Parelle, who held the Valley of St. Martino, would be on their track, and

THE ROCK OF BALSILLE.

they must die on the threshold of their own land, like rats caught in a trap. There was no time for much calculation. Arnaud drew his men together, and briefly told them what they must do.

'Beyond the pass is the vale of Luserna, Angrogna, and the homes we love. The pass is held by two, perhaps three, or even four hundred troops. We must force it, or die. God, who hath helped thus far, will not forsake us now. Ask His aid, Vaudois, not with your lips only, but with your lifted hearts. His strength is with us, as He hath indeed shown us from the moment we left the wood at Nyon. For my part, I can trust Him to give us victory even here. What say you, Vaudois?'

There was a hoarse murmur, a sound more significant than articulate words. The haggard, hungry faces were alight with a living faith, an ardent hope.

'Lead on,' said one in whom they trusted, Montoux, the second in command to Arnaud. 'Lead on! a blow struck swiftly needs not to be struck twice. Two hundred or four, what matters it, since they must be encountered? and so lead on.'

Then Henri Botti stepped to the front, leading Madeleine.

'My wife well knows these hills; here she was reared, and her father's farm stretched yonder up towards Mount Cornan. She crossed the pass this morning at the sunrising, and saw where the enemy lies to bar our path. There is a way, a toilsome and dangerous way truly, but still one that can be trodden by Vaudois' feet, and it will lead us out beyond the crown of the defile, beyond the garrison that holds it against us.'

'It is really so,' said Madeleine, speaking out simply before them all. 'The path is scarcely more than a track for wild goats, but it will serve.'

'Aye, it will serve,' said Arnaud. 'Gaspard Botta, do thou go with thy mother in advance. And as for this maiden——'

'She stays at my side, an it please thee,' interrupted the foster-mother quickly. 'She is my comfort, my charge, my daughter that is to be—Rénée Janavel of Rora.'

The name was enough. Some few who had looked grave at the idea of trusting at so important a crisis to a woman's guidance turned eagerly to look at this girl, the descendant of the old chief Janavel, the man who was waiting even now at Geneva to hear how they had fared. She had something of his bearing too, the same high brow and lofty carriage of the head; ah, yes, it was only fitting that one of the name of Janavel should lead again the warriors of the valleys.

Long afterwards the story was told in Vaudois' homes of how the Pass of Guliano was won; of how the mountaineers crept along the dangerous ways, winning foothold and advancement where it was hard to believe that armed men could go; and always before them was Madeleine Botta, hale and noble in her age and homely dignity; and at her side, with hand held ever out to aid her foster-mother, and eye watchful for each sign of danger, trod the grandchild of their hero, Rénée Janavel. And over and over the tale was repeated how the enemy broke and fled, leaving behind them provision, ammunition, and baggage; a welcome store for the men who came empty and poor in all things save belief in their cause and faith in their God.

Before the sun set the Savoy guard were fugitives on the mountain side, and the Vaudois stood shoulder to shoulder on the Col di St. Guliano, gazing down on the Luserna Valley, the very heart of their fatherland, the goal of their dearest hopes.

There was a renewed strength in Henri Botta's face and mien as he led his wife into the rear, and brought her food from the Savoy stores, and water to bathe her bruised and bleeding feet. And as he tended her and Rénée he turned to kiss the forehead of his adopted child with fervent love and pride.

'God has indeed blessed me, since my old eyes behold once more not only Piedmont, but you!' he said, turning from one to the other, as if he found it hard to believe that they were there in very flesh and blood.

'I have dreamed of you often—of you and of the old house at Rora; as I have dreamed sometimes of God's angels and the fields of heaven. This then is true,' he laid his knotted hand on Madeleine's. 'I verily behold! and the other dream, the heavenly one, is yet to be realised.'

Rénée was crying softly, for very joy and weariness; it was sweet to feel that the lonely struggle was over at last, that she and her mother, Madeleine, were encircled with friendly care, and held safe in loving companionship. The long months and years of hiding and terror were past—the waiting-time had ended in content. And yet the Vaudois had but entered the borders of their Canaan, the victory was yet to be gained, the return was yet to be accomplished.

Arnaud knew that this was so, and his look, though as firm of faith as ever, was grave to sadness as he gazed down on Luserna from the Col di St. Guliano. He knew that hitherto his men had conquered by the wild dash of their onslaught, by the sudden and unexpected way they attacked the French and Savoy troops. This could not continue.

No reinforcements could come from the wasted Vaudois villages, no ammunition could be reckoned on save what they could wrench from the enemy, unless it were the stones from the hill-side which might be used instead of bullets; and as for food they must trust to the half-ripe corn in the fields, and to the produce of such farms as dotted the glens and slopes.

Every day would raise fresh difficulties for them—every mile of ground must be gained by battle, and held by costly strife; and as the struggle swept here and there through the valleys how were the wounded to be tended, or the dead to have Christian burial?

It was no wonder that Arnaud's brow was lined with anxious thought, as his glance swept the country lying before the entrance to the pass. There was stern work in front of his men, and he knew it.

The next day the Vaudois took Bobbio without much difficulty, and they attacked the large town of Villaro in the midst of the Luserna Valley. This latter place was defended by veteran troops, and the duke's general succeeded in thronging into it a large body of reinforcements: and then what Arnaud had foreseen occurred. The Vaudois were beaten back, and obliged to disperse, scattering themselves over the Vandalin range, the very ground where Henri Botta and his sons had retreated before that terrible storm of death and fanaticism in 1686. The papal forces had triumphed then, the mountaineers were driven like autumn leaves before a gale. Was this to be their fate again, now, after such high hopes and glorious imaginings?

Their chronicler writes: 'The defeat at Villaro changed their tactics; henceforth they attacked rarely, and then only convoys, advanced posts, and detached columns. They entrenched themselves in mountainous retreats difficult of access, in natural fortresses easy of defence, while their detachments scoured the country to obtain provisions. It was on the declivities of their mountains, in the centre of their verdant pastures, once covered with their flocks, but now solitary, that they prepared to sell their lives as dearly as might be; decided, as they were, to die in their heritage, on their widowed and desolate soil, or to wring from their prince an honourable peace, and freedom to worship their God.'

But during these trial days they had what they lacked in 1686. Arnaud was their leader, their comforter, their minister. With a courage that never flagged, and a simple faith that was as strong as the sunlight, he preached to them the old enthusiastic trust in the power and the grace of God.

These critical days lasted throughout September, and on the 22nd of October two thousand French troops crossed the frontier, to unite with the duke's forces, and once more 'sweep the valleys clean of heresy.' Then Arnaud called a council, and asked each man if he had any plan to propose, any refuge or resource to indicate. But, for the most part, they recognised the dire necessity of the case, without being able to advise a remedy.

'We can conquer the villages, we can force the passes,' they said sadly, 'but we cannot hold possession of the valleys—we, so poor a remnant, so helpless a company.'

'Neither so poor nor so helpless as those with less righteousness in their cause,' said Gaspard Botta. But he was a young man, and modest, as became his years, therefore his words were almost unheard in the conclave.

It was the leader, Arnaud, who decided on what was to be done. At best it was but a forlorn hope.

Northwards, just within the frontiers of the Vaudois valleys, is Balsille, a village on the Germanasque stream: here Arnaud determined to make a stand. It was a natural fortress, and strong enough, he thought, to be held—at least throughout the winter.

It is a wonderful citadel, this Rock of Balsille: a lofty hill broken into terraces, with fountains of water, and a peak commanding the country for miles around, where sentinels might give timely warning of the advance of the foe. Here they were savagely attacked by the whole strength of the French troops; but the soldiers beat against the place in vain, for the mountaineers had seized every corner of vantage, and had strengthened by earthworks and entrenchments the almost precipitous cliff.

CHAPTER XVI.

THE siege for weeks went on—uselessly. And then, as the days grew cold and dark, the French retired to seek winter quarters. They flung a jibing message to the Vaudois, bidding them have patience, and wait for them there until Easter.

But, meanwhile, how was the Rock of Balsille to be provisioned? The enemy had burned the corn-stacks and granges in the valley, and had carried off every eatable thing to be found. Starvation came very closely into the Vaudois' reckoning in those early winter days, and starvation might have done the work in which the French had failed and conquered the garrison there and then, had it not been for a discovery of Rénée Janavel's.

She had wandered into the valley, past the mill of Macel, and along the banks of the river, seeking something, if it were but a few frost-bitten cabbages, wherewith to make soup for her Mother-Madeleine. She was unsuccessful; the ground had been searched over and over again; not a leaf of salad, not an edible root was to be found. Icicles hung to the idle mill-wheel and fringed the edges of the stream. Long wisps of grasses lay dead and drifted in the water; and the dark sky stooped so low and frowningly that the peak of the Balsille had pierced the clouds and was out of sight beyond the lowering vapours.

Rénée was cold, and she was hungry, yet her eye was bright and her heart was lightsome; privation and suffering were not so hard to bear when safe in the love of those who loved her—the trials of the Balsille were small compared to the silence and the waiting-time in that cave in the vale of Luserna. She wrapped her tattered cloak more tightly round her, and shook the loosened hair from her eyes. She might even have been heard singing to herself as she crossed the wide snow-covered land that stretched by the banks of the river.

Suddenly she noticed a spot where some animal had been scratching in the snow. Could it be straw, grain—eatable, useful *food*, that lay there under the white crust, frozen beneath the snow? She flung herself on her knees, and began to search further and deeper. Presently a burning flush came on her cheeks, an eager light to her eyes.

There was rye beneath the snow. Rye, ripe and plentiful! weighed down, hidden and preserved by the thick white covering that had lain unmelted since the heavy storm of last September. Whole fields of rye! unreaped by the fugitive owners, unguessed at by the troops that had trodden across that white expanse, little dreaming of the treasure beneath their feet.

The girl ran back to the Balsille, and, panting, told her tale. Gaspard's face flushed with proud joy as he heard her; he rejoiced that it was his Rénée that was bringing help to the Vaudois, that it should be the grandchild of Janavel who was the bearer of the best news that could come to the starving and half-desperate people.

'It is our God's granary!' said Henri Botta, solemnly. 'Our Father, who Himself stored His corn for us thus.'

And were not the words true? The God who feedeth the young lions when they cry had not forgotten His servants in the time of their need.

So the silent mill-stones of Marcel revolved once more, and the scent of the dry grain was as fragrance in the nostrils of the mountaineers. 'We shall be ready for the foe at Easter,' they said, and their light-hearted laughter rung out on the wind.

But their case was too grave and their position too perilous for a few acres of rye to be their salvation. When Easter came they were still holding the Balsille; but as Arnaud called them together for the daily service of prayer, he noted how their ranks had shrunk, and he saw how sickness had reduced the strength of such as still called themselves fighting men.

The foe returned in early spring; a foe numbering now no less than twenty-two thousand! Arnaud and his feeble garrison could muster but about six hundred! surely an insignificant garrison to call forth such an armament for its reduction. Cannon were planted on the opposite hill; batteries were cast up on all sides. The Balsille must be taken now, were the Vaudois as obstinate as the *barbets* their enemies had scoffingly likened them to. A flag of truce was sent to them, and they were summoned for the last time to surrender.

Arnaud's answer is historical. 'We are no subjects of the King of France,' he said. 'We cannot treat with his officers. We are in the heritage left us by our fathers from times unknown; by the aid and grace of the Lord of Hosts we will live and die therein. Discharge your artillery; our rocks will not be terrified, and we will listen to the thunder with calmness, should there be but ten of us left!'

The defiance was as lofty in tone as ever, but yet the heart of the man who sent that proud answer had been brought very low. His trust did not fail him, nor his submission to God's will, but he had begun to think that it must be this will of God that he and his men should die there on the hills of their country, and that the race of the Vaudois should perish from the earth. 'Even so, Father, since it is good in Thy sight!'

On the 14th of May they saw the Balsille could no longer be defended. Flight only remained; and once more they must begin the weary wanderings amongst caves and holes in the rocks, chased as David was chased by Saul on the hills of Palestine. Covered by a dense fog, they crept through the French lines, a woeful wreck and remnant, flying to their hill hiding-places, afraid lest word or step should betray them to immediate slaughter. Southwards they fled; down through Prali towards the mountains of Angrogna.

'Mother,' said Rénée, 'this wild journeying will kill thee. We women can never keep up with the march of our troops. Is it not better to stay here where we stand? we can but die.'

MESSENGERS APPROACHING.

But Madeleine laid her hand against her lips. 'Courage yet, dear child. It is nearly over now.'

Nearly over—aye, but in another sense than that she meant.

On the 18th of May two men met the flying Vaudois. They were messengers from Victor Amadeus, and messengers to them.

A strange message they bore. England, Germany, Holland, and Spain had formed a coalition against Louis XIV., and had called upon the Duke of Savoy to decide at once whether he would join their alliance or hold to his friendship with France. He had decided; and on the side of the strongest; therefore the French were now his enemies; and he sent to ask whether Arnaud and his mountaineers would enrol themselves on the side of Savoy, and help to drive Louis' men back across the frontier. If Arnaud consented, the valleys were to be placed there and then under his protection and control.

Could it be true? 'Protection,' 'control.' Strange words in the ears of the handful of hunted outcasts who were flying for their lives. But to enforce the news and prove its truth the Piedmontese garrison of La Torre sent out food and gifts of clothing, which were indeed sorely needed; and other messengers came from the duke, repeating the same tale and demanding instant reply. And presently—most conclusive proof of all—their minister, Montoux, and others who had been carried prisoners to Turin, came hurrying to meet them in transports of joy.

Yes, it was true! God had remembered His promise, and had been faithful to His word. The trust of the Vaudois had not been in vain, the struggle was over—the victory was won!

Before many months were past the Vaudois were re-established in their homes; from the east and west they came, flocking homewards to their land won for them by Arnaud and his heroes. Or, rather as they themselves would say, the land restored to them by the grace of their Father in heaven.

The sharp endurance, the agony, the exile—all, all was past, and for the years to come they and their children's children might lift humble hearts in thankfulness that God had honoured them by letting them bear such witness for His truth.

The charter of their freedom was given at last. The valleys were their own; their faith was secure.

...   .

A white-walled cottage in Rora stood smothered in vines, and resonant with children's voices. Here Rénée, sweet-eyed as of old, albeit of matronly air and manner, watches for Gaspard's coming from his work as her busy hands ply distaff or needle, and her foot keeps the rocker of the cradle moving in time to her song.

It is a song in which an aged voice joins now and again as Mother Madeleine catches the well-known burden of the words—a song which the Vaudois have chanted since the hour of their 'Glorious Return'; not the 'Psalm of Strong Confidence,' but the song of their triumph.

'If it had not been the Lord was on our side
When men rose up against us,
Then they had swallowed us up quick, and the stream had gone over our soul:
Blessed be the Lord, who hath not given us
As a prey to their teeth!
Our soul is escaped as a bird from the snare.
The snare is broken, and we are escaped!
Our help is in the Name of the Lord,
The Lord who made heaven and earth.'

APPENDIX.

THE INSTRUCTIONS GIVEN TO HIS COMPATRIOTS BY JOSHUA JANAVEL, WHO WAS TOO OLD TO ACCOMPANY THEM ON THEIR 'GLORIOUS RETURN.'

THE Lord not permitting me, to my great sorrow, by reason of my infirmity, to follow you, I considered it my duty to neglect nothing for the good of my poor country: therefore I give you in writing my ideas as to the course you should take on the way, and in your engagements and attacks, if the Lord mercifully bring you to your mountains, as I hope, and I pray God with all my heart that He may prosper everything to His glory and the re-establishment of His Church. I beg you, therefore, to take in good part the contents of this letter.

If our Church has been reduced to such an extremity, our sin is the real cause thereof. We must more and more every day humble ourselves before God, and earnestly crave pardon ... ever having recourse to Him; and when troubles arise be patient, redouble your courage, so that *there may be nothing firmer than your faith*. Therefore doubt not that God will preserve you and accomplish your projects to His glory and the advancement of the kingdom of Jesus Christ.

As soon as you reach the enemy's territory, you must seize three or four men of the place, wherever you find them: then you must make them march with you from place to place, and when you reach some part where there is danger of alarms, you must send one of these men with one of your own to give notice to the peasants to trouble themselves about nothing, and that you will do them no harm or injury, if only they let you pass.... And if you want anything you must pay them fairly.

You must behave as prudently as possible for the sake of your neighbours, the Swiss Lords, who should be your friends.

Moreover, as to the management of the war, provided that God in His mercy allows you to go whither you desire, you must, every one of you, fall on your knees, raise your eyes and hands to heaven, your heart and soul to the Lord in earnest prayer, that He will give you His Spirit, and enable you to choose the most capable amongst you to lead the others.

In the evening you must all gather together to offer prayer to God. You must place numerous sentinels, using the most timorous of your soldiers for the evening and throughout the night, and the boldest and most expert towards daylight.

When you see the enemy approaching, let them draw as near as possible: fire at first upon the officers, make no ill-timed discharge, and be prompt in recharging your arms, and, if possible, have bullets which exactly fit the bore of the gun, to ensure straight firing.

When you pursue or make a search for the enemy, put soldiers in the field to attack the flanks of the troops, but never allow the head to advance without notice from the flank; in this way you will all be safe, and Christ's Church also, *provided you be faithful Christians.*

In every encounter take great care to spare innocent or useless blood, so as not to have to answer for it before God; and, above all, be not overcome by fear or by anger; then will the sword of the Lord, as well as His grace, be with you, and he who trusts in the living God shall never perish.

Whoever passes over to the enemy, unless he be taken prisoner arms in hand, must be punished with death. He shall have the liberty of choosing the persons by whom he is to be shot.

Sentence of death must be passed upon anyone who remains on the field of battle to plunder the enemy before orders from the captain.

After the first battle it is desirable that your officers change clothes with the more poorly clad members of their company. While on the march there is no need to grant any quarter to prisoners.

Trust neither the letters nor the words of the enemy: and it is when they desire to confer that you must be most on your guard.

When you make an attack you must have ambuscades in the flank, and after making an advance you must fall back, so that the enemy may pursue you; when the engagement occurs in the ambuscades, you must face about, and so you will make many dead and wounded, for *such are the fruits of war.*

Spare converted families (*catholisées*), for otherwise God would be grieved.

If God grant that you reach your mountains, which I hope, you must first know where your place of retreat is to be. If you are only six or seven hundred strong, you must attack simultaneously the Valley of Luserna and the Valley of St. Martin; but first fix your retreat, which should be in the Valley of St. Martin, the *Balciglia*, and in the Valley of Luserna, *Balmadaut*, *l'Aiguille*, and *La Combe de Giausarand*, which was the ancient retreat of our fathers.

Always keep sentinels on the tops of the mountains, so as not to be surprised from the Pragela side, and keep the passes clear from one valley to the other. On the Col Julien place a guard composed of men from each valley

—half from one, half from the other.

As for you others of the *Balciglia*, he continues, you are all men of strength and used to toil; therefore spare no pains in well fortifying this point, which will be a very strong retreat for you.

In case you are attacked by a large number of troops, you must withdraw altogether to the most convenient places, such as *Balmadaut, Sarcena, La Combe de Giausarand*, and *l'Aiguille*; but leave the *Balciglia only at the last extremity*. They will not fail to tell you that you cannot hold out for ever, and that all France and Italy will turn upon you rather than you should succeed; but *say that you fear nothing, not even death, and that if the whole world were against you, and you alone against the whole world, you fear only the Almighty who is your Protector.*

To regain possession of your valleys, he says, you must first seize that of St. Martin. To make a successful attack, you must form three companies,— one to occupy the mountain tops, the second to keep the Bridge of the Tour (near Pomaret), and the third must be divided into two, to invest Perrier. It is very necessary to take Perrier, as otherwise no assistance or retreat is possible without discovery.

As to the Valley of Luserna, the highest mountain must be reached, and promptness must be exercised in sending half of the soldiers down the rivers to cut the bridges, then to stand their ground in planting ambushes in suitable and narrow places. The Bridge of Subiasq must be strongly guarded, to prevent the carrying off of cattle and provisions.

As to the town of Bobbio, I do not believe that the enemy will encamp there. As to Villar, I will tell you by word of mouth what I think. I will not commit it to writing. Tour must be invested at night, and completely surrounded by fires, so that the smoke may serve as a screen from the fire of the fort. As to St. Jean and Angrogna, I cannot tell you all the plans proposed, and therefore you must act according to circumstances.

As soon as you have entered the valleys you must put up the ministers, doctors, and wounded in the Serre-de-Cruel, and when the town of Bobbio is taken they should withdraw to Sarcena; and when Villar is taken, they should go to Pertuzel, and when Tour is taken to Rua-de-Bonnet or to Taillaret. Finally, when Pramol, Angrogna, and Rocheplatte are taken, they must be removed to Pra-du-Tor, whence they will bestow their care and good advice upon the people of both valleys.

W. RIDER, AND SON, PRINTERS, LONDON.